Praise for David Rosenfelt

WITHOUT WARNING

"[A] riveting . . . suspenseful page-turner."

—*Publishers Weekly*

"[Rosenfelt] excels at creating fascinating plots and telling his stories with crisp writing that's a pleasure to read. The plot of his new book has a relentless sense of urgency that captures readers' attention early on and never lets go."

—*RT Book Reviews* (4 stars)

"Spooky. Creepy. Edgy. Shuddery. What more could anyone want? Highly recommended for readers craving that elusive 'something different.'" —*Booklist*

AIRTIGHT

"The tension is palpable, and the pages fly by in this riveting stand-alone thriller . . . The voice here is every bit as engaging as in the Carpenter novels, with enough humor to lighten the story without diminishing the suspense. And the ending is a real shocker. Sure to appeal to fans of Harlan Coben and Robert Crais." —*Booklist*

"As usual, there is plenty of irony, humor [illegible]e, and affection here . . . Rosenfelt is, inde[illegible]l; you will burn through this novel [illegible] stop and totally rapt. It's [illegible]*com*

"Perfectly controlle[illegible] *[illegible]ews*

"Keep[s] you on the e[illegible]."

—*Criminal Element*

HEART OF A KILLER

"A full-blown suspense chiller." —*Publishers Weekly*

"Rosenfelt has crafted another terrific thriller that will keep the reader up late at night." —*Huffington Post*

"Warmhearted, satisfyingly inventive and almost too clever for its own good. Why isn't Rosenfelt a household name like Michael Connelly and Jeffery Deaver?"

—*Kirkus Reviews*

ON BORROWED TIME

"An absolutely irresistible hook . . . No one who picks up this greased-lightning account will rest till its finished."

—*Kirkus Reviews* (starred review)

"Outstanding . . . Anyone who enjoyed Dennis Lehane's *Shutter Island* will love this thriller."

—*Library Journal* (starred review)

"Excellent. All will marvel at the way Rosenfelt builds suspense." —*Publishers Weekly* (starred review)

DOWN TO THE WIRE

"Dynamite . . . Sly humor, breathless pacing, and terrific plot twists keep the pages spinning toward the showdown."

—*Publishers Weekly* (starred review)

"Rosenfelt's Andy Carpenter novels are known for their breezy storytelling and humor . . . This one eschews humor to focus on the actions of ordinary people faced with extraordinary trials. It also employs a whiplash plot turn . . . an engaging suspense tale." —*Booklist*

"A terrific plot and a gripping narrative."—*The Toronto Sun*

"I am raving about this book . . . a page-turning thriller."
—*Deadly Pleasure*

DON'T TELL A SOUL

"Stellar . . . Rosenfelt keeps the plot hopping and popping as he reveals a complex frame-up of major proportions with profound political ramifications both terrifying and enlightening." —*Publishers Weekly* (starred review)

"This fast-paced and brightly written tale spins along . . . *Don't Tell a Soul* is a humdinger."
—*St. Louis Post-Dispatch*

"High-voltage entertainment from an author who plots and writes with verve and wit . . . Rosenfelt ratchets up tension with the precision of a skilled auto mechanic wielding a torque wrench." —*Booklist* (starred review)

"Rosenfelt has earned his crime-novelist pedigree."
—*Entertainment Weekly*

"He delivers a fast, inventive stand-alone thriller you'll never put down." —*Kirkus Reviews*

"[Rosenfelt] has pulled together a cynical political thriller that rings true in this age of terrorism, media hype and Washington scandals . . . it's an enjoyable tale."
—*Minneapolis Star Tribune*

"Rosenfelt's first stand-alone novel is a riveting thriller that should boost him to best-seller status . . . Compelling twists and turns, a lightning-fast pace, and breathtaking suspense make this a harrowing ride . . . The book deserves a wide audience." —*Library Journal* (starred)

ALSO BY DAVID ROSENFELT

ANDY CARPENTER NOVELS

Who Let the Dog Out?
Hounded
Unleashed
Leader of the Pack
One Dog Night
Dog Tags
New Tricks
Play Dead
Dead Center
Sudden Death
Bury the Lead
First Degree
Open and Shut
Outfoxed

THRILLERS

Without Warning
Airtight
Heart of a Killer
On Borrowed Time
Down to the Wire
Don't Tell a Soul

NONFICTION

Lessons from Tara: Life Advice from the World's Most Brilliant Dog
Dogtripping: 25 Rescues, 11 Volunteers, and 3 RVs on Our Canine Cross-Country Adventure

BLACKOUT

DAVID ROSENFELT

St. Martin's Paperbacks

BLACKOUT

For information address St. Martin's Press, 175 Fifth Avenue, New York, NY 10010.

ISBN: 978-1-250-05532-3

Our books may be purchased in bulk for promotional, educational, or business use. Please contact your local bookseller or the Macmillan Corporate and Premium Sales Department at 1-800-221-7945, ext. 5442, or by e-mail at MacmillanSpecialMarkets@macmillan.com.

Printed in the United States of America

St. Martin's Press hardcover edition / January 2016
St. Martin's Paperbacks edition / October 2016

St. Martin's Paperbacks are published by St. Martin's Press, 175 Fifth Avenue, New York, NY 10010.

10 9 8 7 6 5 4 3 2 1

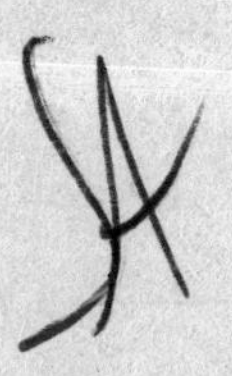

For Dick Mayer and Dave Kramer,
who have spent their lives defining "serve with honor"

NATE ALVAREZ WANTED TO SCREEN THE CALL.

Actually, he wanted to throw the phone on the ground and stomp on it until it stopped ringing permanently. There were times in his life that he would have done exactly that, but Nate was thirty-seven years old, and in recent months there had been faint signs that he was starting to mature.

Caller ID told him that it was his partner and friend, Doug Brock, who was trying to reach him. They hadn't talked for the past two days, and Nate had been hoping that Doug had seen the light and curtailed his actions. The ringing phone was a likely indication that the lack of communication was just a short break in an otherwise rapid descent.

Before the two-day pause, each conversation had been the same, and Nate had grown tired of it. Doug would tell him that he was making progress, that he was close to wrapping up the investigation triumphantly. He wouldn't give details, just would say that Nate would be blown away by what Doug was unearthing. Nate would respond that Doug should not be investigating at all, and that he was jeopardizing what was left of his career, after having pretty much destroyed his personal life. That message had absolutely no chance of getting through.

But Doug wasn't just Nate's partner, he was also his best friend, and Nate knew that he was the only person who could calm him down during the frequent times that Doug's frustration started to peak. More importantly, he was the only person with any chance to keep Doug from doing something he would regret for the rest of his life.

Doug was a loose cannon, always had been. Sometimes it helped him on the job, and sometimes it didn't. What it did was thrust Nate, his partner, into the role of seasoned, level-headed veteran. It was not a role that Nate was particularly well suited for.

So the answering machine kicked into action, but then Nate relented and picked up the phone himself, because that's what partners and friends do. The delay had the unintended effect of causing the remainder of the call to be recorded. "Hey, Doug. What's going on?"

"I got him, Nate. This time I got him. You . . ."

Nate could hear the elevated stress level in Doug's voice. He had become used to it, but this time it was more severe than usual. Once again he would have to talk him down off a ledge that was becoming higher and more precarious. He interrupted with, "Doug, come on, you can't keep doing this."

"Shut up, Nate, and listen. You've got to get down here with backup, and you need to notify the FBI."

"FBI?" This was a new twist, and an unwelcome one. "Why?"

"It's much bigger than we ever thought, Nate. And I've got it all."

There was probably nothing Doug could have said that would have been more surprising. "Where the hell are you?"

"Find Congers and—"

"Hey!" was the next word that Nate heard through the phone, but it wasn't Doug's voice. After that there was a rattling, as if the phone were dropped, and then the unmistakable sound of two gunshots . . . then a few seconds later, two more.

And then the only sound Nate could hear was his own voice, screaming into a dead phone.

EVERY CELL PHONE HAS A GPS BUILT INTO IT.

The phone company, and therefore any government entity with subpoena power, can learn where a phone is at all times, including retroactively. That ability is used in police work with great frequency.

So the first thing that Nate did after screaming in vain for Doug to answer him was call headquarters and ask to speak to Jessie Allen.

"Jess, it's me."

"Hey, Nate, I thought you were off today?"

"Yeah. Jess, we need to trace Doug's cell phone. It's urgent."

"What did he do now?" she asked, her voice turning considerably colder.

Nate didn't even want to take the time to answer the question. "Urgent . . . please . . . just do it as fast as you can."

Even expedited, it would take at least an hour to get the information, and Nate was fairly sure that by the time they got it, they would no longer need it. He wanted to get up, to go drive somewhere and do something, but he had no place to go. So he paced, and he worried, and he waited.

He knew the proper thing to do was to call Captain Bradley, but for the moment he resisted. There was nothing more that Bradley could do right now, and if by some wild chance Doug should be okay, the call would put him in even more trouble within the department than he was already in. Nate didn't want that, of course. So that loyalty, which he understood was probably misplaced, is what prevented Nate from making the call.

He also had no idea what to tell the FBI, or Dan Congers; Doug never got to tell him why they needed to be involved. Congers was the NJ State Police liaison to the Joint Terrorism Task Force, so bringing in the FBI and Congers simultaneously was at least consistent.

So for the time being, he would wait.

He didn't have to wait long. Twenty minutes later the phone rang, and it was Jessie. But she wasn't calling with GPS information. "He's been shot, Nate," she said, her voice breaking. "The call just came in."

"Is he alive?"

"I don't know, the person who found him didn't know. If he was moving, or talking, they would know, and they would have said so."

"Where is he?"

"The Peter Pan. It's a motel—"

He interrupted her. "I know where it is. I'm on my way."

"So am I," she said, and she hung up the phone.

He knew she shouldn't be there, professionally or emotionally, and he knew just as surely that there was no way he was going to stop her. So instead he got in his car and headed for the Peter Pan Motel on Route 4 in Teaneck, New Jersey, just fifteen minutes from his house in Elmwood Park.

By the time Nate got there, it seemed as if the motel was hosting a police convention, and all the attendees had arrived at once. There had to be twenty-five cars, most with flashing lights, filling the small parking lot and surrounding area. Nothing draws the police faster and in greater numbers than when one of their own is down.

The Teaneck Police Department was out in force, but they had already been relegated to a secondary position. This was a state cop that had been shot, and the state cops were not about to have anything less than total control. So the locals were the ones manning the perimeter, and they were the ones who stepped aside to let Nate through when he showed his badge. Of course, showing the badge wasn't really necessary, since at six foot four, 290 pounds, Nate was well known and very recognizable.

Based on the concentration of officers, Nate immediately realized that the center of the action was in the rear of the two-story motel, so that's where he went. He scanned the scene for Captain Jeremy Bradley, and found him on the second floor, outside near the railing.

Nate also saw the vehicle he was hoping not to see,

the coroner's van. It felt like a punch in the gut; they didn't just wander onto crime scenes, they had to be summoned. And they weren't summoned unless they were needed.

Nate took the stairs two at a time, not easy for a man his size, and then started walking toward Captain Bradley. Bradley was talking to two other detectives, but moved away from them and toward Nate when he saw him coming.

"Captain . . . ," was all Nate could say as he braced for the news.

"He's alive, Nate. On the way to the hospital."

The relief Nate felt was palpable, but there was much more to learn, and to dread. "How bad is it?"

Bradley shrugged. "No way to know. He took a bullet in the shoulder, and one in the leg; neither seemed too bad. But he either fell or jumped from this railing, and sustained head injuries. He was unconscious."

Nate pointed to the coroner's van. "Why are they here?"

"Two fatalities," Bradley said. "A couple in their forties; they were guests and staying in the room almost directly below where Doug went over the rail."

"Were they involved?"

Bradley shook his head. "Doesn't appear so, but that could change. Most likely wrong place at the wrong time."

"Do we know how it went down?"

Bradley shrugged. "Just speculation. It's possible that Doug was in that room over here; the lock was broken.

Maybe the shooters walked in on him, and he got by them and tried to get away. But there's no way to know for sure." Then, "You got any idea what Doug was doing here?"

Nate nodded. "In a way I do," he said, and he proceeded to describe the call.

Bradley listened without interrupting, and when Nate was finished, he asked, "Did he mention Bennett by name?"

"I don't think so. I think he said, 'I got him.' But there's no doubt who he meant." Then he realized the chain of events, and he said, "You know, I probably have a tape of the call, because I was screening it, and picked up when I heard his voice."

"Good, let's get that as soon as possible. But why would he want you to bring in the FBI?" It was a logical question; local cops, even state cops, have a natural resentment for the Feds, who are prone to pushing the locals out of the way. Doug's antipathy for them was common knowledge, but in any event, Bennett's alleged criminal activities were not federal. There had to be something new that Doug believed he had uncovered.

"I didn't get to ask him, and he didn't get to tell me," Nate said. "I assume he wanted me to find Congers for the same reason."

"I'll ask Congers if he knows anything about it."

Standing against the upper railing, they both saw Jessie down below, working her way through the milling officers. "You'd better get down there and talk to her," Bradley said.

"Yeah. She's going to have a tough time with this."

"Hey," Bradley said, "after what Doug did to her, if you hadn't told me about that phone call, she'd be a suspect."

"I'M GOING TO THE HOSPITAL," JESSIE SAID, ONCE NATE *updated her on the situation.*

"I can't imagine they'll let you in to see him," Nate pointed out.

"I don't want to see him, but I want to be there."

Nate nodded his understanding, and then went back to confirm that he wasn't needed at the scene, and that he could go with Jessie to the hospital. "Okay," Bradley said. "Call me and let me know his condition; especially if he's alert and talking."

Nate arranged for one of the officers to take Jessie's car home, and then he drove her to Hackensack Hospital, where there was already a heavy police presence on the scene. The cops had not been assigned there, and had no real purpose, other than the fact that they wanted to be around for their injured brother. It was a show of solidarity, though it certainly wasn't done for show.

Nate and Jessie entered the hospital and found out that Doug was in surgery on the fifth floor. At the nurses' station they were not able to learn anything about his condition, other than the fact that a neurosurgeon named Dr. James Carmody was performing the operation, and that the affected area was the brain.

They didn't realize it, but they took different things from hearing that news. For Nate it was a major negative: brain surgery was a terribly serious thing that conjured up thoughts in his mind of a lifetime that might forever be horribly impaired. Doug was not someone who dealt with limiting physical problems well; a few years earlier when he'd broken his ankle badly and was bedridden for two weeks, he made everyone he knew contemplate suicide.

Jessie's reaction was very different than Nate's: to her it meant one thing above all else, that Doug was alive.

So they took up a vigil in the waiting room, having been promised that the doctor would come out and discuss the situation with them at the conclusion of the "procedure." They sat for at least forty-five minutes without saying a word. Nate was very worried, but he couldn't even imagine what was going through Jessie's mind.

Jessie had joined the force four years ago, but it was almost exactly a year to the day since she and Doug had gotten engaged. They seemed to be the perfect couple, if there could ever be such a thing. She had gotten Doug to calm down, even to act the part of an adult on occasion, and Nate was among those amazed at her accomplishments.

But six months ago, Doug had suffered a personal tragedy that shook him to his core. He had volunteered for a few years as the baseball coach for a local Babe

Ruth League team and had gotten close to one of his players, a fourteen-year-old named Johnnie Arroyo. Doug had become a father/mentor figure for him, and would take him out to things like ball games and movies.

Johnnie was an orphan in foster care, and his foster family no longer wanted him. Doug was anxious to adopt him, and Jessie gave the idea her blessing. She cared for Johnnie as well, and wanted him to have a real family and loving atmosphere, which she was sure that she and Doug could provide.

Then came the night that Doug and Johnnie were walking from the local diner to Doug's car. A car pulled up alongside them, the window opened, and someone inside opened fire. Doug saw it coming and leaped to protect Johnnie, but two bullets wound up hitting the young man. One wound was inconsequential, but the other pierced his heart, killing him instantly. Doug was not hit, though he was certain that the killers had been after him and that he knew who had sent them.

The tragedy and subsequent guilt sent Doug into a tailspin. Professionally, his unsuccessful actions to avenge the killing resulted in his suspension from the force, a suspension that had begun six weeks ago, and was said to be indefinite. Personally, he withdrew from friends and family, and the person who bore the greatest brunt of it was Jessie. Nate and Jessie became helpless allies, reduced to watching as Doug continued his descent.

Jessie was devastated by Johnnie's death as well, but rather than band together with her in their shared grief,

Doug withdrew. He simply could not accept anything that might help him deal with the pain and guilt, and he shut himself off from everyone around him. Three weeks ago he had broken off his engagement to Jessie, telling her that he no longer loved her. The truth was he hated himself.

Her response, no surprise, was intense hurt and anger, which she threw at him in that final conversation. She had not seen or spoken to him since, a distance made easier by the fact that he was suspended and not coming in to work. Now there was a chance that they would never see or talk to each other again.

"You want something to eat?" Nate asked finally. "There's a cafeteria downstairs." The tension was making him hungry; pretty much everything made him hungry.

"No, thanks. I want to be here in case the doctor comes out."

"I could bring you something."

"Not hungry, Nate. But you go ahead."

He shook his head. "I'm on a diet . . . I'm three weeks in."

"How much have you lost?"

"I didn't weigh myself this morning, but as of yesterday I was down eight ounces."

She smiled; the first time since hearing about Doug. "I can see it; you're looking good."

Nate sat back down, but a few minutes he later wandered over to nearby vending machines. He came back with a diet soda, a package of cookies, and two bags of pretzels.

He held up the cookies and pretzels. "These are no sugar added, and these are nonfat. You want some?"

Before she had a chance to decline, she saw a doctor come through the door and walk to the nurses' station. Something told her that this was the surgeon, and she stood up just as he turned and walked toward her. Neither she nor Nate could read the expression on his face.

"I'm Dr. Carmody. Are you Mrs. Brock?"

The question was momentarily jarring to her. "No," she said. "I . . ."

Nate reached them and interrupted. "We work with Doug; he's my partner. How is he?"

"At this point it's too soon to say. He came through the surgery very well."

"So he's going to be okay?" Jessie asked.

"He's suffered a severe traumatic injury to his brain. There was a great deal of swelling, and we surgically relieved the pressure that it caused. At this point he is in an induced coma."

"What does that mean?" Nate asked.

"We are giving him drugs to keep him in a comatose state. The goal is to reduce the amount of energy and activity in his brain, giving it the time and space to heal. We want his brain to rest."

"Will it heal?" Jessie asked, cringing in anticipation of the answer.

"There's really only one way to answer that," Dr. Carmody said. "We'll know when we know. But getting through the surgery this way is a huge step."

"So you're hopeful?" Jessie asked, desperate to extract something positive from this conversation.

Dr. Carmody smiled. "I'm always hopeful," he said, and then walked away.

Since there was no prospect of Doug waking up from a coma that was induced, Nate and Jessie left the hospital. He dropped her off at her house, promising to call if he got any updates, and then drove on to his house.

It was just a few minutes later that he saw the e-mail.

THE MEETING WAS HELD AT THE FBI OFFICES IN THE *Federal Plaza Building in Manhattan.*

Captain Bradley and Nate were ushered into the office of Wilson Metcalf, who introduced himself as the special agent in charge. Also there was Dan Congers, who had come in from the task force offices in Newark. Metcalf described himself as being in charge of the case. Nate and Bradley, to that point, hadn't even realized there was a case, at least not as far as the FBI was concerned.

After the brief introductions, Metcalf said, "Gentlemen, we are joined electronically for this meeting by Assistant Director Peter Cantrell and some of his colleagues in Washington. So please remember to smile for the cameras. Now let's get right to it."

The lights in the room dimmed slightly as one of the agents in the rear of the room fiddled with some buttons. A large screen seemed to come out of the wall, and on it was the e-mail that Nate had found in his inbox when he came home from the hospital. The only words typed in the body of it were "Nate, run this ASAP."

"Lieutenant Alvarez, please tell us whatever you can about this e-mail. Leave nothing out."

Nate shrugged. "Not much to tell. It was sent to me by my partner, Doug Brock. It was sent about an hour before he got shot, but I didn't see it until much later that night."

Metcalf asked Nate to describe the chain of events, starting with the phone call and ending in the hospital. Nate was sure that the agent already knew all of it; he was either simply getting the story on some record, or going through it for the benefit of the unseen viewers in Washington.

The first question he asked when Nate was finished was, "Did he give you any indication at all why he suggested you call in the FBI, as well as Lieutenant Congers?"

"No. He didn't get a chance to. All he said was 'I got him.' Haven't you heard the tape?" Nate asked, knowing that he must have.

Metcalf ignored the question. "Do you know who he was referring to when he said, 'I got him'?"

"I can't say for sure, but my assumption was Nicholas Bennett. You're familiar with him?"

"Of course," Metcalf said. "Why did you make that assumption?"

"Because Doug has been after him for two years, and his people killed a teenager that Doug was really close to."

"So why is he walking the streets?" Metcalf asked.

"Doug was trying to change that," Nate said, and Bradley added, "We've had something of an evidentiary problem. Witnesses, when they exist, seem to prefer living to talking. But we're making progress."

"What did you do when you got the call?"

"I called an officer named Jessie Allen; she's in our tech division, and I asked her to run a GPS location check on Doug's phone. Before we got the response, she called to tell me Doug had been shot."

Next Metcalf turned to Lieutenant Dan Congers. State police forces, and most big-city ones as well, have people in their organization assigned to the JTTF, the Joint Terrorism Task Force. Congers was one of those handling that assignment for the Jersey State Police.

One of his functions was to deal with both the state police and the task force, to make sure that each side knew what the other was doing. But he got his daily marching orders from the task force, and that's where he spent most of his time. It required an ability to manage the egos of both the Feds and the state police, who had a natural distrust of each other.

"Any idea why Brock wanted Lieutenant Alvarez to find you?"

Congers had gone over this with Bradley, and was sure the information had previously been conveyed to Metcalf, but he repeated it. "Not really. He had called me a couple of times the week before. He wanted to know if Bennett had any involvement in international arms smuggling."

"How did you answer that?"

"First I advised him to be careful; that he was on suspension and could be making his situation worse. Then I told him I had no information about Bennett being involved in that world. I have since checked deeper, and that answer holds. But I couldn't do anything other than speculate as to why he wanted to reach me the day he was shot, and it would be uninformed speculation at best."

"Speculate away," Metcalf directed. "We can assign it the proper weight."

"Okay," Congers said. "Before I joined the task force, I was a thorn in Bennett's side, and that's putting it mildly. I spent a lot of time trying to put him away, so I know a lot about how he operates. So with whatever he learned, or thought he learned, about Bennett, he might have thought I could be helpful."

Metcalf nodded to the man working the computer, and the cursor on the large screen clicked on the "attachment" icon on Nate's e-mail. A photograph of a man appeared. It was very dark, most likely taken at night, and a little blurry, but the man's face was recognizable. "This was attached to the e-mail," Metcalf said, a statement more than a question.

Nate nodded. "Yeah, it was obvious that the photo was what Doug wanted me to run, so as soon as I saw it, I put it into the national database."

"And then?"

"And then we wound up sitting here, answering a thousand questions. Who is this guy?"

Metcalf avoided the question and instead asked another of his own, this time directed at Bradley. "Brock was conducting this investigation on his own?"

An annoyed Nate spoke up before Bradley could answer. "You know, this is feeling like a one-way street. How about you answer my question? Who is the guy in the picture?"

Metcalf ignored him and kept his focus on Bradley. "Captain?"

"It seems like a reasonable question," Bradley said, sticking up for Nate. "Who is he?"

Metcalf paused for a moment, then seemed to relent and said, "His name is Ahmat Gharsi. Born in Yemen, but based wherever there are people that he feels deserve killing. He has very strong connections throughout the Middle East."

"He's a terrorist?" Nate asked, an obvious question that he regretted as soon as he asked it.

"He literally wrote the book. Is Brock being properly guarded in the hospital?"

Bradley nodded. "We have two officers there, twenty-four/seven."

"Good. Now, was Brock conducting this investigation on his own?"

"Lieutenant Brock was on suspension. He was certainly not doing anything authorized by our department, nor was he consulting with me."

Metcalf turned to Nate, who shrugged. "Me neither. But just to be clear, Doug is right about Bennett."

Metcalf referred back to the image of Gharsi on the screen. "Based on the background or anything else you see, can you tell where this photograph was taken?"

"What background? It's all dark. Can you enhance it better?"

“This is already enhanced,” he said. “Our experts say that it was likely taken through a glass window.”

“Sorry, I wish I could help, but I have no idea where that was taken.”

“We need to find Gharsi,” said Metcalf. “And just as importantly, we need to know why he is in this country.”

“I’ll bet Doug knows,” Nate said. “But unfortunately, right now, he’s not talking.”

"THE DOCTOR SAID THERE'S A GOOD CHANCE HE WON'T *remember what happened," Nate said.*

He was having lunch with Jessie, fulfilling a promise to keep her updated on what was happening with Doug's condition. Nate was talking with his mouth half-stuffed with a meatball hero; Jessie was occasionally poking with little interest at a salad.

"Permanently?" she asked.

He shrugged. "I don't know, and I don't think the doctor does either. But the FBI is putting pressure on him to bring Doug out of the coma."

"Why the FBI?"

Nate was under strict instructions not to reveal what he'd learned in the meeting with the Feds. "I can't say, Jess."

"Doug's not in any trouble, is he?"

"You mean besides being in a coma?"

"You know what I mean, Nate."

"Yeah, sorry. I don't think he's in trouble, but it all

depends on what he says if he wakes up." He quickly corrected himself. "When he wakes up."

Nate looked down at his empty plate and frowned. "You think another meatball hero would be bad for my diet?"

"Probably," she said.

"Maybe there's another way to get thinner besides losing weight. Maybe I can get taller."

She smiled. "Good idea." Then, "What's the doctor going to do?"

"Nothing. Not until he's ready. He says he'll do what's best for Doug, and he doesn't give a shit what the FBI wants. I like his style."

"Did he say how Doug is doing?" she asked.

Nate nodded. "Yeah, he still says he's pleased with the progress. Swelling is way down, and he thinks he actually might cut off the drugs that are inducing the coma. But he wanted me to know the FBI pressure has nothing to do with it."

"And then Doug will wake up?"

"Not necessarily, but he might. The doctor wasn't sure; he keeps saying 'We'll know when we know.' But if I know Doug, he'll stay asleep, just to piss us off."

"Any progress on the investigation?"

"Not so far; but I'm not on it, Jerry Bettis is lead detective. The room was registered under a fake name, and nobody admits to seeing anyone or remembering anything."

"Because they're afraid of Bennett?" she asked.

He shrugged. "That's a safe bet. I'll ask him about it when I see him."

"When are you going to see Bennett?"

He looked at his cell phone, which three years prior replaced his watch. "In about forty-five minutes. When we put out the word we wanted to talk to him, he offered to come in. A goddamn model citizen."

"Why is he doing that?"

"Probably would rather deal with us than the Feds."

"The Feds are actively involved with the investigation of the shooting at the motel?" she asked.

"I'm sure they must be, but they haven't interfered with us yet. I expect them to move in at any time."

"But you can't tell me why."

Nate could see that while she may have understood his promise to keep the confidence, she was also slightly offended that she, as a cop herself, was not being trusted with this information. "Sorry, Jess. I can't. If it's any consolation, I don't know a hell of a lot. The Feds really aren't much into sharing."

Nate and Jessie went back to the state police barracks, and he stopped in at his office before going into the interview room. There was a message from the hospital that the doctor was in fact going to stop the drugs that were inducing Doug's coma at five o'clock that afternoon. Left unsaid was what Nate already knew, that there was no telling what might happen after that.

Nicholas Bennett and his attorney, Richard Mayweather, showed up precisely on time and were led into the interview room where Captain Bradley and Nate were waiting for them. Someone not familiar with them could never have known which was the lawyer and which was the criminal. Both were dressed and groomed impeccably, which Bennett had long been known for.

Bennett's appearance was particularly deceiving. He was fifty-three years old, graying, tall and thin. He looked more like a refined patron of the arts than a person who had clawed his way up the criminal ladder in northern New Jersey. And ironically, he was in fact a patron of the arts, as well as a contributor to many charitable causes.

As age, disloyalty, and especially the justice system had wreaked havoc on the dominant old-time crime families in New Jersey, a vacuum was created. Bennett was one of a number of people attempting to fill that vacuum, and while he may not have been the favorite on the morning line, he was the one who was ultimately successful, the last man standing.

That success came from his possessing three major assets. First was money: Bennett came from a wealthy family and was a successful businessman in his own right. He owned a large number of apartment buildings in New York and New Jersey that were cash cows. Second, he had an understanding of organizational structure, an underrated factor in criminal enterprises. Third, he was totally and utterly ruthless; to mess with Nicholas Bennett was to die a certain and very unpleasant death.

Various competitors possessed some of these assets, but none had all three, and therefore they dropped away one by one, until Bennett finally prevailed more than six years ago. He had spent the time since consolidating his power and reputation; not an easy thing to do.

If Bennett were a sports fan, he might liken his position to that of a defending Super Bowl champion. Everybody tries to knock the champ off of the pedestal, and though Bennett was at the top of the organized crime heap, none of his competitors were willing to cede him the position for life.

So they'd come after him, and he'd used up men and resources to fight them off. Money had become a particular problem of late. Like the employees of any legitimate company, Bennett's people expected to be paid for their loyalty. It was an expensive proposition.

Neither Bradley nor Nate expected this interview to be at all productive; Bennett was far too smart to incriminate himself in any way. Typical of his self-protectiveness was his insistence that the interview be recorded, so nothing he said could be misrepresented at a later time. Bradley had readily agreed to the condition in advance, but Bennett, not taking any chances, had Mayweather operate his own recorder as well.

"I just want you to know," Bennett said, "that my thoughts and prayers are with Lieutenant Brock. I understand that he was grievously injured."

"He'll be touched by your concern," Nate said.

Bennett smiled. "I'm not sure the recording devices can successfully convey the sarcasm in your tone, Lieutenant Alvarez, so allow me to note it. Even though Lieutenant Brock has for some reason conducted something of a vendetta against me, I bear him no ill will."

The interview did not go downhill from there; it just went nowhere. Bennett said that he had no idea who was responsible for the shooting and had ten witnesses who would testify that he was nowhere near that motel at the time.

Bradley and Nate had known that they would accomplish very little, and they were right.

They never laid a glove on him.

I AM IN A HOSPITAL; THAT MUCH I'M PRETTY SURE OF.

There are tubes in my arms, and one in my nose, which I imagine is to help me breathe. The room is filled with machines, displaying numbers that must be my vital signs and other statistics that doctors are accumulating about me. They're blinking and beeping a lot, which doesn't tell me anything. I can't tell the difference between good beeping and bad beeping.

I don't know what hospital I am in, or why I am in one at all. Something must have happened on the job, but it is almost physically painful to try and remember what that might have been. I feel like I am covered with gauze; there's a general haze over me that I can't seem to push through.

Maybe I am drugged.

Maybe it's not a hospital at all.

I hear someone coming, but I can't turn to see who it is. I think there may be bandages on my head, but I don't know if that is why I can't turn. It could be that I just don't have the energy.

"Hello, Doug. How are you feeling?"

He looks like a doctor, and he knows my name. I didn't see him come in, but then again, I don't even know where the door is. I don't answer him, because it seems like it will take too much energy to summon my voice. I also don't know what I would say, because I really have no idea how I am feeling.

Except for tired. I'm quite sure that I am very, very tired.

Behind the doctor are three other people. I don't know if they are also doctors, or nurses, or whatever. They're all dressed in white; I am surrounded by a world of white. Each of them looks concerned, and they're all wearing smiles that seem to be forced for my benefit.

"My name is Dr. Carmody. You're in Hackensack Hospital; do you know why you're here?"

I don't know why I'm here, but I don't seem to have any desire to tell him that. Maybe I won't have to; maybe he'll just tell me.

"You were hurt, so you had an operation, but you're much better now." He smiles. "And you're going to be just fine."

Everyone behind him is still smiling and nodding and looking sincere. I've never seen any of them before, so I don't know if I can believe them. Whatever happened to me must have been very bad if that many people are crowded into this room. I want to know how long I've been here, but I just can't seem to will myself to speak.

"We're just going to poke and prod you a little, Doug. It's nothing that will hurt. And then you can sleep some more. Will that be okay?"

He must take my silence as a yes, because he comes over and presses some parts of my body, and then shines a light into my eyes. It seems really bright in my right eye, but much less so in the left one. I should tell him that, but I don't.

I feel something on my arm, like from a blood pressure machine, though I didn't see or feel them wrap it around me. Maybe it was already there. When it's finished squeezing, I don't feel them removing it. There also seems to be padding of some kind on my legs, and they must be attached to a machine, because they squeeze my legs at odd intervals.

"Very good," the doctor says, apparently pleased with whatever he's learned. "Doug, there's a button here, right next to your arm. If you need anything, or if you feel anything unusual or painful, just press that button, okay? Someone will come help you."

Okay, I think in silence.

He smiles again. "Now we'll let you get some rest. You're tired."

Yes. I am.

AHMAT GHARSI DID NOT TRUST NICHOLAS BENNETT.

That in itself was a cause for neither surprise nor concern; Gharsi could not remember the last time he trusted anyone. He was quite certain that if he had, he would have been dead long ago. In his business, you simply did not trust anyone except yourself.

The fact that Gharsi judged Bennett's truthfulness and honor to be unreliable was, in any event, a non-issue. In the world in which people like Gharsi and Bennett operated, it was understood that those qualities were, if anything, impediments to success. The motto they lived by was "Don't trust, but verify."

It was amusing to Gharsi that Bennett was considered to be so tough and ruthless by the Americans. If he were on Gharsi's turf, he would not last an hour.

What really concerned Gharsi was Bennett's competence, or lack of same, since he would have to rely on it if the operation was going to be successful. Certainly the relationship was not off to an auspicious start; the fiasco at the motel had the potential to destroy that operation before it began.

The news that the cop was not dead was certainly unwelcome. At this point there was no way to know what he had learned, but that answer would come soon enough. If the cop had discovered what was going on, and had revealed it to the FBI, then Bennett would soon be arrested, and Gharsi would have to start all over again.

What Bennett did have was organizational ability and access to that which Gharsi most needed . . . people. They were accustomed to violence, and most important, they were people who felt passionate about nothing except money.

These were not the people that Homeland Security generally worried about. The Feds were relentless in finding ideologues, people who were intent on hurting the United States. For that type of person, killing and wreaking havoc was an end in itself.

Gharsi could recruit such soldiers, and had in the past, and they would provide total loyalty and a willingness to sacrifice their own lives. The problem was that the United States security apparatus was so complete and intrusive that they could simply not fly under the federal radar.

The people Bennett was committed to providing would be different. They would be willing. And they would be anonymous. And under Gharsi's tutelage, they would be deadly.

But a lot of work had to be done before the job could be complete, and the situation with the cop had caused

Gharsi to change his plans. Rather than go back and work on that end of things, he would stay in the United States and manage this side of the operation.

Gharsi had no idea if the FBI knew that he was in the U.S. They probably did not, but he had to operate as if they did. He knew quite well that the way to avoid being detected by people was to surround himself with people. So he was going to stay in New York City, and with perfect fake identification and some minor cosmetic changes in his appearance, he would not be found by the authorities, whether or not they were looking for him.

Eventually they would learn that he was there.

After the fact.

But that was one side of the coin, and on the other side was Nicholas Bennett, a man that Gharsi underestimated at his peril. Bennett viewed Gharsi as a meal ticket; whatever government was backing him seemed to have unlimited funds to do it. This was money that Nicholas Bennett needed, and that he was going to get his hands on.

Ahmat Gharsi would learn that Nicholas Bennett was a force to be reckoned with, and one he would not be able to handle.

After the fact.

THE NAME TAG SAYS HER NAME IS DARLENE AZAR, AND *she appears to be my nurse.*

She has been in a bunch of times, sometimes with the doctor, and sometimes not. She takes my blood pressure and temperature, and changes the bags that seem to be dripping fluid into my arm. Looking out the window, I think it's dark out, so maybe she's the night nurse. The difference between night and day isn't that significant to me at this point.

She always gives me a cheery hello, but doesn't ask questions like the doctor does. I like that about her. I don't feel like answering questions; I would rather ask them. And when I get up the strength, I will.

"How long have I been here?" I ask out loud, surprising myself in the process. At least I think that was me; my voice sounds different, somehow strange.

She turns in surprise, and moves toward me. "I'm sorry . . . I couldn't hear you."

She's going to have to listen better, because I sure as hell can't talk any louder. "How long have I been here?"

"Let me call the doctor. He can answer all your questions."

"No. Please . . . just tell me."

She nods and says, "Five days," which surprises and pleases me; for some reason I thought it was going to turn out to be much longer. She continues, "You're doing great; the doctors are very happy."

I must have fallen back asleep, because next thing I know it's light out, and a nurse named Heather is in the room. She sees that my eyes are open and says, "Good morning." She's every bit as cheery as Darlene.

My plan is to answer her, but I seem to be on some kind of tape delay, and before I can speak any words, she has left the room. I'm not surprised when she comes back a couple of minutes later with the same doctor I saw before.

"Well, good morning, Doug. Darlene said you were a regular talking machine last night."

I don't say anything, so he says, "How are you feeling?"

The truth is that I'm feeling a little better; the haze is starting to clear a little bit. "Okay," I say, and I'm again surprised at the sound of my voice. I wonder if something happened to my throat.

He nods vigorously. "Good. You're making great progress." He pulls a chair up next to my bed. "If you're up to it, I'd like to ask you a few questions. It's part of my job, and will help us care for you. After that, I'll try and answer any questions you might have."

"Okay," I say, and I think I nod as well.

"Good. Let's start by squeezing my arm, as hard as you can."

It feels like I barely can exert any pressure at all, but he tells me I did well, and has me do it with my other hand. The effort feels like running a marathon, without the panting.

"What's your full name?"

"Doug Brock. Douglas Anthony Brock."

"Excellent. Where do you live?" He's looking at something on a clipboard as he's asking these questions.

"At 432 East Thirty-third Street, Paterson, New Jersey."

"What do you do for a living?"

"I'm a New Jersey state cop."

"Are you married?"

"No." I'm sure he's asking me these questions to test my mental faculties, and it's actually helping me think more clearly.

"How old are you?"

"Twenty-six."

He hesitates a moment, then asks, "Who is the president of the United States?"

"George Bush."

"Father, or son?"

"Son. George W."

"Do you know today's date?"

"No."

"How about the year?"

"It's 2005."

"Who won the Super Bowl this year?"

I have to think about that for a second. "New England.

They beat Philadelphia." I can actually picture in my mind the end of the game, when the Eagles, down two scores, didn't even bother to go into the no-huddle. Since I dislike the Patriots, I remember screaming at Donovan McNabb to hurry up.

"Very good, Doug. I'll let you rest now."

"How did I get hurt?" I ask.

"You came in here with two bullet wounds, one in your shoulder and one in your leg, both of which are healing well, and will not cause any lasting damage. You also suffered a serious head trauma, apparently from a fall after you were shot."

"Who shot me?"

"I don't know the answer to that. When you're well enough, I'll notify some of your colleagues that you are available to talk. I'm sure they'll be far more knowledgeable about it than I am. My entire focus is on helping you get better."

"Okay," I say, and at this point I can barely keep my eyes open. "Maybe tomorrow."

"THIS IS THE AREA OF THE BRAIN THAT IS AFFECTED."

Dr. Carmody said this as he pointed to an area on what he said was an MRI of Doug's brain, backlit by a display case in the darkened room. His audience consisted of Captain Bradley, Dan Congers, Nate, and Special Agent Metcalf, who remained in charge of the FBI/Homeland Security side of the investigation.

None of the four law enforcement officers could detect anything unusual in the area of the brain that Dr. Carmody was pointing to, but they had no interest in pointing that out. If he said the brain was affected, then the brain was affected. Metcalf also knew that FBI-hired neurosurgeons would be poring over the MRI to double-check Carmody's work.

Carmody flicked on the room lights and moved to sit behind his desk. "We still need to do some further testing, including an AMI, which is an autobiographical memory interview. But I think at this point I can say, without fear of contradiction, that Lieutenant Brock has what we call retrograde amnesia."

Bradley spoke first. "So he doesn't remember the events surrounding the shooting? Or is it more than that? What are we looking at here?"

"Retrograde amnesia is very patient specific. Patients have no recollection of events starting with the trauma and going back in time. Some can have all of their memory erased, but more often the loss only goes back a specific number of weeks, months, or years."

"And in his case?" Bradley asked.

"He believes it to be 2005. His ability to recall before that time is very much intact, but after that it has been wiped away."

"So he knows his name? That kind of stuff?" Nate asked.

"Yes, in these situations the basics about the person remain unaffected. For instance, his personality will be the same, as will his understanding of the world around him. The same is true for his physical abilities and motor skills; for example, he'll know how to drive. All that is stored in a different section of the brain." He pointed to a couple of areas on the MRI. "Here, and here."

He continued. "What is missing is his recollection of episodes, experiences he has had. In Doug's case, he simply cannot recall any episode or experience since 2005. For him, it is as if the last ten years never happened."

Agent Metcalf asked, "Will he recover those memories?"

"Probably, but not definitely. Every case is different. He might recover some, but not others, and the recovery will not necessarily be chronological. But there is absolutely no timetable."

Metcalf tried again. "Is there anything medically you can do to speed the process up?"

"There are things we can and will try. We typically use Alzheimer's drugs, and we increase the amount of thiamine in the body. There is disagreement in the medical community about the effectiveness of all this. Personally, I haven't seen very many positive results. Hopefully this time will be different."

"How about hypnosis?" Bradley asked.

Carmody shook his head. "Unfortunately, that only has the potential for success when the trauma is psychological and emotional rather than physical. Look, the bottom line is that patients either get better, or they don't. It can happen spontaneously all at once, or the memories can come back slowly, or not come back at all."

"So what can we do?" Bradley asked.

"My advice would be to return him to his normal life and job as soon as he can handle it physically. Don't bombard him with memories, let him reconnect naturally. Certainly do not remind him of traumatic experiences, physical or emotional."

"That's it?" Nate asked.

Carmody nodded. "That's it. Let nature take its course."

DOUG SPENT MOST OF THE NEXT TWO DAYS SLEEPING.

During his waking hours, further tests were conducted, none of which did anything to change the diagnosis. The gunshot wounds were by that point on the way to being healed, and Doug had regained some of his strength. Under the watchful eye of a physical therapist, he was even able to walk down the hall with no ill effects. Physically, he was going to be fine.

Without anyone telling him why, he was not given access to newspapers, and was told the television in his room wasn't working. He therefore remained unaware of his mental condition, and the doctors determined that it would be best for a friend to be there when they broke the news. It might be less traumatic that way.

Dr. Carmody was making all the decisions, independent from the outside pressure that he was feeling. The FBI, as represented by Agent Metcalf, was particularly impatient. The idea that Doug had information about a known terrorist—a terrorist who might be in the area—was something they couldn't afford to take lightly. They didn't tell Carmody anything other than that there was an urgency to the process, but they and he knew the clock was ticking.

Actually, the pressure was not as great as it might have been, because the Bureau neurologists were supportive of Carmody's position. These things could not be rushed; to do so would be unproductive at best, and counterproductive at worst.

Dr. Carmody finally gave the okay: Doug Brock was ready to take the first step toward reentering his life.

Nate arrived at nine o'clock in the morning and waited in Dr. Carmody's office for word from Doug's nurse that he was awake and ready for visitors. It was an hour and twenty minutes before that call came, and another twenty before Carmody became available.

"You ready?" Carmody asked.

"Ready."

DR. CARMODY COMES IN TO SEE ME FOR THE FIRST TIME *today.*

He's been showing up twice a day, once in the morning and once at night. He doesn't do much to examine me physically, but he asks a million questions. He seems to be trying to confirm that I'm okay mentally. I feel like I am, but for some reason I don't appear able to convince him.

This time he's brought somebody with him, a huge guy who is dressed nothing like a doctor, but who sort of looks familiar to me. Maybe he's been in here before, and I was too out of it to remember him clearly.

The big guy smiles as he comes over to me, and says, "Hey, Doug; how ya doin', man?"

Now I can place the face, but not the body. It's a guy that's on the force with me. "Nate?"

He smiles. "You remembered."

"Did you gain a lot of weight?"

"Thanks a lot, pal."

"You going to tell me how I got here, Nate?"

He starts to answer, but then turns to Carmody. "Doc?"

Now it's Carmody's turn to come over to the bed; he's on my right, and Nate is on my left. "Doug, first of all, I want to give you an overview of your condition."

I don't like how that sounds; I thought he already told me about my condition. But there's nothing I can do but wait to hear what he has to say.

He continues, "As I've told you, you suffered a fairly severe trauma to the head. The good news is that it is healing wonderfully, even better than expected, and there is no reason you cannot go on to have a long, healthy, productive life."

"But . . . ," I say, trying to prompt him to drop whatever the hell bomb he's going to drop.

He smiles. "But there is a complication. You have what we call retrograde amnesia. While your capacity to make new memories is unimpaired, it has at least temporarily resulted in you forgetting a chunk of your recent life."

"How much?" I ask.

"It's 2015, Doug."

"You're shitting me." I look toward Nate, hoping that he's laughing and in on the joke, but he's not.

"I've had ten years to gain the weight, pal."

"Ten years gone? Just like that? Am I going to get them back?"

"There's a good chance you will," Carmody says. "But I can't make any promises. Just relax, take it one day at a time, and let it happen."

I can't seem to wrap my mind around this, and

I'm having a feeling of panic. "Ten years? It's not possible."

Nate smiles a forced smile. "Believe me, you didn't miss much. They were shitty years. By the way, we've been partners and good friends for the last six."

I ask Carmody a bunch of questions about my condition, and he answers them all, but it's nothing I enjoy hearing. He either has no idea what is going to happen, or he does and he doesn't want to tell me. I'm rooting for the former.

"I want to get out of here," I say. "If I've lost ten years, I don't want to lose any more."

Carmody nods. "There's no reason you can't be released. You just need to take it easy; you've been through a lot."

"You're going to come live with me for a while," Nate says.

"Why? Am I homeless?"

"Nah. You've got a pretty nice apartment. We'll go by there to get your stuff."

"I don't want you living alone," Carmody says. "At least not until you're at full strength. Of course, you can always stay here."

There's no way I'm doing that, so I turn back to Nate. "You still live alone? You didn't get married?"

"I've been turning down proposals all the time."

"I'm not married, am I? Do I have three kids and a dog?"

"No."

I think I'm relieved to hear that, but I'm not sure. "Okay, your place it is."

Carmody nods with apparent satisfaction. "Good, I'll set it up for tomorrow. If you don't feel strong enough, we can push it back."

I shake my head; there's no way I'm staying here a minute longer than necessary. "I'll be ready."

"Pick you up at nine in the morning," Nate says, and they both leave. They seem to be telling the truth about this retrograde amnesia thing, but it still seems hard to believe. I need to get out in the world so I can see for myself.

Big day tomorrow.

DOUG WAS UP AND DRESSED WHEN NATE ARRIVED.

He was tired; just the act of showering and dressing took pretty much all the energy he had. But he was anxious to get out of the hospital. The nurse insisted that it was hospital policy for Doug to be brought downstairs in a wheelchair, and he didn't resist. He appreciated the ride.

When they got down to the lobby, he asked the guy pushing the chair to stop in front of a newspaper vending machine. Sure enough, the date on the front page confirmed that it was 2015. The scam couldn't be that detailed, he realized. This had to be real.

He waited as Nate pulled his car up to the front. It was a 2013 Crown Victoria, owned by the department. Inside was a rifle mounted between the driver and passenger seats, but that was not what drew Doug's attention. He was focused on the electronics, the computer screens and communications systems, which were like nothing Doug could remember seeing. "What the hell is all that?" he asked.

"Modern tools of the trade," Nate said. "Your car is exactly the same. But don't worry, the trunk is full of old-fashioned things like weapons and tear gas. The kind of stuff you love."

Once they were out on the road, any lingering doubt Doug had that Nate and Carmody were telling the truth was soon dispelled. The cars looked different, and even though Doug had always had a keen interest in cars, there were some he had never seen before.

Some of the malls they passed had new stores in them; billboards advertised products he had never heard of. Then Doug reached into the bag of personal belongings the hospital gave him when he checked out. He held up a device. "What's this?"

"It's your iPhone."

"Like a cell phone?"

"Boy, have you got a lot to learn. I'll show you how it works later. You also have an iPad and iPod touch. You like Apple stuff."

"If it's Apple, why isn't it called an aPhone?" Doug asked, as he fiddled with the device a bit. In the process he accidentally activated Siri. "What can I help you with?" her computer voice asked.

"What is that? Is she talking to me?"

Nate laughed. "She's your best friend, and the only woman you'll ever meet who gives a shit about what you want. Hey, you want to go to your place and get some stuff, or if you'd rather, we can get you to my place and I'll go pick it up? You can rest that way, which might be a good idea. You look like shit."

"No, I'll go with you," Doug said. "I can't believe I'm saying this, but I want to see where I live."

They drove to an apartment building in Hackensack called Royal Towers. It was familiar to Doug, but not as a place where he'd ever lived, but rather because there was a bar across the street called The Crow's Nest that he had been to a bunch of times. The bar was still there and looked the same; for some reason he was comforted by that.

He was quiet as he and Nate got out of the car, and he stumbled as they started walking. Nate went to grab him, but he righted himself and waved him off. They reached the elevator and got on. "What floor?" Doug asked.

"Four."

They rode up to the fourth floor and got off, with nothing whatsoever looking familiar to Doug. Nate reached into his pocket and took out a key, then put it in the door. "We keep copies of each other's keys," he explained. "Just in case."

"You mean in case ten years of my life gets wiped away?"

"Something like that."

The door across the hall and slightly down from Doug's apartment opened and his neighbor, Bert Manning, came out. He took a step for the elevator, but then saw Doug and Nate.

"Hey, Doug . . . how ya doin'? I heard you had some trouble."

"A little bit, but I'm fine, thanks."

Manning seemed as if he wanted to say something, but looked at Nate and decided better of it. Instead he offered his hand to shake, and said, "I'm Bert Manning."

"Nice to meet you, Bert," Nate said.

Bert then turned back to Doug. "So you're okay?" he asked. "Everything's okay?"

Doug nodded. "All good."

Manning hesitated again, and then nodded and headed for the elevator.

Doug and Nate entered, and Doug walked through the apartment, silently taking it in. It seemed inconceivable to him that he had ever lived there, though he did recognize many of the things as his own. The kitchen table, the recliner chair, the Phil Simms jersey hanging on the wall . . . there was more than enough to convince him that this was, in fact, his home. Or was his home, before he lost his mind.

"This is so fucking weird," he said, more to himself than to Nate.

They loaded up two suitcases with clothes and Doug went into the bathroom to get some toiletries. He saw himself in the mirror, the first time since he had gone to the hospital. "You look old," he said to his reflection. "Shit, you are old." Then he realized why his own voice sounded strange; it was ten years older than the last time he remembered hearing it.

When he went back into the living room, Doug asked, "Do I still play softball?"

"Nah. You hurt your arm breaking up a fight in front of a bar. Now you play squash."

"Squash?"

Nate nodded. "Yeah. According to you you're pretty good. We're all set, huh? We can come back if we need anything else."

Nate grabbed the pair of suitcases, and Doug started to follow him toward the door. He stopped when he noticed a picture of himself and Jessie on the beach with what looked like a resort hotel in the background. "Who is she?" Doug asked.

"An ex-girlfriend."

"She's great looking. What happened?"

Nate shrugged. "Just didn't work out."

"Too bad, I guess. Unless she's a serial killer or something."

"She is definitely not a serial killer."

They drove to Nate's house in Teaneck, which Doug remembered, having been to a couple of barbeques there. It was the house that Nate grew up in, and stayed in when his parents moved down to Florida. It looked exactly like it had looked all those years before.

"You've certainly done a lot with the place," Doug said.

Nate nodded. "Yeah, it's really coming around."

"So who shot me, Nate? That's something I'd sort of like to know."

"We don't know, pal. If we did, they'd be in jail."

"What were the circumstances?" Doug asked.

"Get some rest," Nate said, looking through the drapes out the window toward the front. "You'll come to the barracks tomorrow, and we'll go over everything with the captain."

Doug walked over and saw what Nate was looking

at. It was a state police car that had parked in front, with two troopers in the front seat.

"What are they doing here?" Doug asked.

"Let's put it this way: whoever shot you, we want to make sure they don't shoot you again."

WAKING UP EVERY MORNING I HAVE THE SAME SEN-*sation.*

Things seem normal . . . I seem normal . . . and my first thought is that it isn't possible. There's no way I could have lost ten years of my life.

I'm pretty pissed off about it. It's like I was in a coma all that time, as if I never lived those years at all. I'm already realizing that life is all about memories; it's the way we keep score. It doesn't matter if the tree makes a sound when it falls in the forest; it only matters if anyone remembers it.

This iPhone thing I have is amazing. Last night I was trying to find a way to get my memory back, so I figured I'd check out what's happened in the world and see if that would help. So Nate showed me I could just ask the phone to have this Siri woman tell me what happened in any particular year, and before I knew it she was giving me all this information.

I read it, I know it's true, but it doesn't seem possible. How could I not remember my Giants beating the Patriots in the Super Bowl? Twice! An African-American runs for president and wins, and it slips my mind?

I tried to focus on that stuff, and a bunch more that I read, and I tried to force myself to relive it. But I didn't come close; none of it rings any kind of bell.

I'm nervous today. Nate is going to take me to the barracks, and I'm going to see all these people who will know me, and who work with me. But chances are I won't have a clue who most of them are. I'm going to feel stupid, and helpless.

"When we get there we're going to go into the meeting room," Nate tells me, once we're on the way.

"What for?"

"The captain wants you to meet everyone at once; get it out of the way. So everyone not on duty will be there. He thinks it will be easier on you that way. Sounded like a good idea to me."

"Who's the captain now?" I ask.

"Name is Bradley. He's a good guy; you'll like him. You liked him, even though you think he's an asshole, and he thinks you're a pain in the ass."

"Why does he think that?"

"Probably because you're a pain in the ass."

The state police barracks looks pretty much like I remembered it. It was built just a year ago as measured in my life, which means 2004, and it's really eleven years old. It's held up well.

We get inside, and there is a woman at the reception desk. "Hey, Doug, welcome back. Good to see you," she says, a smile on her face.

"Hello," I say. "Nice to see you too."

As soon as we get past her, Nate says, "Her name is Nancy."

"Now you tell me."

He brings me to the conference room, and when I open the door I see about thirty people, maybe two-thirds of them men, sitting and standing there. They all get up when I walk in, and in smiling bunches they make their way slowly over to me. The whole thing seems to be choreographed, as if someone told them how to act in front of the weirdo.

Each one says hello, and tells me their name. They obviously know about my condition, so I don't feel a need to explain. I feel badly that I don't know them, but it's way down on the list of things I feel badly about.

When I get to the middle of the line, I see a face I recognize. "Hi, Doug, good to see you. I'm Jerry Bettis."

"I know you, Jerry. From the Academy."

He smiles. "Yeah, amazing we both made it out of there."

The next person says, "Hello. I'm Jessie Allen."

I think this is the woman that I saw in the photo on my night table, the one that Nate said I went out with. I didn't realize that she was a cop. She looks every bit as good as she does in the picture. She shakes my hand in a sort of robotic way. If there is any remaining warmth between us, I'm not picking up on it.

"Hello, Jessie, nice to meet you," is the best I can come up with, and she seems to bite her lower lip as she walks on.

Once I've met all my old friends for the first time,

Nate brings me to the captain's office. Like everybody else, he greets me with a smile on his face, as if he's treating a lunatic with serene kid gloves.

"Doug, I'm Captain Bradley. Good to have you back. Have a seat."

"Thank you, Captain. Good to be back, even though I don't remember leaving."

We sit down and Bradley gets me coffee. Even without a memory, I am pretty sure that he's doing so for the first time ever. Getting coffee is not a typical captain function, and I don't think that would have changed if I was out of it for a hundred years.

"I just want you to know that you are being reinstated to the department with full back pay."

"What rank am I?" It's a question I hadn't thought to ask Nate.

"Lieutenant. You were promoted three years ago."

I nod. "Why was I suspended in the first place? And while you're answering that, it's time someone told me the circumstances behind my getting shot."

Bradley and Nate shoot glances at each other, and then Bradley nods. "It's all related," is how he starts. He reaches for something on his desk; it's a photograph of two men, and he holds it up for me.

"Do you recognize either of these guys?"

"No."

"The one on the left is Nicholas Bennett. He's today's version of what used to be called the head of a crime family. We've gotten close to him a few times, but he's so well insulated that we've never been able to pin anything on him."

"He looks like a businessman," I say.

"That's how he sees himself, but his businesses include drugs, prostitution, money laundering, gambling, and murder. He's been a main target of ours for a long time, but you became obsessed with him."

"Why?"

He hesitates and says, "Because you're a cop, and you give a shit. But you went too far, you harassed him, and you pushed him into a cabinet. He bruised a rib, lodged a complaint, and we had no choice but to suspend you. Restraint has never been a particular strong point of yours."

I feel like he's not telling me something, but I ask him whether that's the case, and he denies it. I point back to the photo. "Who is the guy with him?"

"Name is Luther Castle," Bradley says. "Bennett's right-hand man, his enforcer when all else fails. Castle is as bad as it gets; he's Bennett without the bullshit slick façade."

"So what was I doing when I got shot?"

"We'd sort of like to know that as well. You were supposed to be sitting at home, riding out the suspension, but you weren't following the drill. I didn't know it, but you were out on your own, trying to bring Bennett down. One day you made this phone call to Nate."

He presses a button on a recorder, and I hear my voice.

"I got him, Nate. This time I got him. You . . ."

Nate's voice is next. "Doug, come on, you can't keep doing this."

"Shut up, Nate, and listen. You've got to get down here with backup, and you need to notify the FBI."

"FBI? Why?"

"It's much bigger than we ever thought, Nate. And I've got it all."

"Where the hell are you?"

"Find Congers and—"

"Hey!" is the last thing either of us says, and then there is the sound of gunshots. It's very weird to hear myself getting shot, to say nothing of having no memory of it.

"Where did this happen?"

"The Peter Pan Motel."

I know where that is, but I don't ever remember being there. "How did you find me?"

"Well, Nate asked Jessie to trace the GPS on your phone, but before she got the answer, a call came in. I think one of the guests in the motel found you and called nine-one-one."

"So Bennett or one of his people is the shooter?" I ask.

Bradley shrugs. "That's the best guess, but no way to be sure."

"Who is Congers, the guy I mentioned in the call?"

"Dan Congers. He's a state cop, used to be a buddy of yours. Now he's assigned to the Joint Terrorism Task Force. And there's one more thing." He shows me another photograph. "This is Ahmat Gharsi; Homeland Security says he's an international terrorist, and a big-time one."

"How is he involved?"

"You sent an e-mail to Nate with this photo attached, an hour before you got shot. You wanted him to run it. Homeland Security is rather anxious for you to remember why."

The impact of this hits me all at once. Something major may be going on, and the answer might well be inside my head. I just have no way to access it.

"Shit," I say.

Nate speaks for the first time since we came in the office. "You got that right."

GHARSI HAD NEVER BEEN TO A USED CAR LOT BEFORE. His visit to this one in Garfield was not meant to correct that oversight, and was not something he had on his bucket list. It also wasn't to buy a car, used or otherwise.

Gharsi wasn't worried about being seen and identified by other customers; this was a special visit arranged at two o'clock in the morning. And he wasn't greeted by one of the normal salesmen, but rather by Nicholas Bennett.

Bennett had sent a driver to pick him up, and the man was waiting in the parking lot to bring him back to the city. Gharsi was looking out at the sixty or so cars in the lot, at this point lit only by moonlight, when Bennett and Luther Castle approached him.

"Are you in the market for a car?" Bennett asked. "I'll give you a good deal."

Gharsi smiled. "I'm interested in many of them, and I have no intention to bargain. I am paying what you Americans call top dollar."

Bennett returned the smile. "Then let's go inside."

They walked inside to the showroom, a rather dingy place not conducive to upscale buyers. "You own this business?" Gharsi asked.

"Not officially, but it's fair to say I have an interest in it."

Castle smiled, but didn't say anything. His job was not to speak, it was to let his boss do the speaking, and to make sure his boss's words were heeded.

"How many cars do you sell?" Gharsi asked.

"More than you would think. But this place has other purposes."

Bennett and Castle led him into the back, which was the service area and body shop. They walked through that into a large garage-like room that had no apparent function other than to house a dozen fairly large cars. They were nondescript, not likely to attract undue attention, and each was at least five years old.

Gharsi walked slowly through the room, peering into each of the cars, opening some, and looking in all of the trunks. As he did so, Bennett said, "They are all untraceable. The VIN numbers have been removed, and it will be impossible to tell their history, recent or otherwise."

Gharsi saw no reason to question Bennett's statement, since he didn't care if it was accurate. Once these cars had done their job, it didn't matter to him at all if they were traced. If they were, it would be Bennett and others who would be in the cross hairs; Gharsi would be long gone.

"What about the license plates and identification?" Gharsi asked.

"All will be completely legit and up to date. No chance of attracting attention."

"And the people driving them?"

"That is being worked on," Bennett said. "And it will not be a problem, provided the money is there, and the escape is assured."

Gharsi smiled. "Excellent, then we will do good business together."

TO THIS POINT, THE MEDIA HAD ONLY REPORTED THE *basics of the story.*

They had been told, and they conveyed to the public, that Doug had been investigating a domestic disturbance at the motel, and was gunned down in the process. The fleeing shooter had also killed two innocent bystanders as he made his escape. To this point no suspects had been identified, and a special tip line was set up.

They had no idea, and therefore could not report, anything about the apparent involvement of Bennett and Gharsi. Some outlets knew that Doug had been on suspension for overzealous actions on the job, but they bought the line that he had been previously reinstated. No one in the media even speculated that the suspension and shooting were in any way connected.

There were follow-up reports on Doug's successful surgery and recovery, but the fact of his memory loss remained a closely guarded secret. Bradley, his superiors, and Homeland Security were in total agreement on the need to keep that information in house. If Bennett knew that Doug might someday reveal what he knew, it would be a motivation to target him. If he believed that Doug had already revealed it, or did not know anything in the first place, then killing him would serve no purpose.

All of this planning and strategizing was done without the benefit of one specific piece of information: they had no idea that Bennett already knew all about Doug's condition.

The department kept disseminating information about Doug through press releases. It was all done in a matter-of-fact manner, as if there was nothing particularly unusual or urgent about any of it. The last release simply stated that Doug had recovered well, and was returning to work.

The actual return to the job was to be treated internally with a similar "business as usual" approach. Doug would work regular hours, provided he was physically able to do so, and he would perform his normal functions. As before, Nate would be his partner, and would be able to monitor him and prevent him from overdoing it.

The theory, which the doctors signed off on, was that gradual reintroduction to his former life would have the most chance of enabling him to regain his memory. There were certainly no guarantees, and success with this approach was usually spotty at best, but it was the best way they had to handle it.

Bradley explained this all to Doug with Nate in the room, so that everyone would be clear on it. "This is what is best for you, Doug, and it's also the approach most likely to help you remember. It's a win-win."

"Makes a lot of sense, Captain," was Doug's response.

Bradley smiled and nodded. "Good, let's do it." He stood up, indicating the meeting was over.

Once they had left the office, Nate said, "You good with all this?"

"No chance."

"I had a feeling you weren't."

"Why is that?" Doug asked.

"Because the doctor said your basic personality wouldn't change. And 'Makes a lot of sense, Captain' doesn't quite fit your personality. 'Kiss my ass, Captain' would be a little closer."

"Good, because it's not going to happen the way he thinks."

"Let's go downstairs," Nate said. "When I get stressed I need a donut."

They went down to the cafeteria. Doug sat at a table while Nate went and got a coffee for him, and a coffee for himself. He also got a jelly donut and a chocolate glazed one.

"I didn't want a donut," Doug said when he saw the tray.

"Good, because they're both mine. I've got a feeling I'm going to be really stressed. Let's hear it."

"Here's how I see it. This guy Bennett knows that I know something, and he's afraid I'm going to remember it."

"No way he can know you have amnesia."

Doug shook his head. "Bullshit. How many people in our barracks? Fifty? Every one of them knows it."

"None of them would talk to Bennett."

"They don't have to. They talk to their wives, or girlfriends, or buddies. Before long the whole world knows it; it'll probably be in the goddamn *Bergen Record.* Bennett has to be smart and tied in, or he'd be making license plates by now. So if he doesn't know the real deal already, he will soon enough. But I'm betting he does, and it's safest to assume that he does."

"So?" Nate asked, though he knew where this was going.

"So I'm not going to be handing out traffic tickets and breaking up bar fights, while this guy figures out the best way to kill me. Because he's got to know that killing me is the only sure way for him to survive."

"So you're going after Bennett?"

"Hopefully, we're going after Bennett together. But if you don't want to, I understand, and I'll do it on my own."

"You already tried that," Nate pointed out.

"And I obviously made some progress; I just don't remember what it was."

"You know I should discuss this with the captain, right?"

"That's your call," Doug said.

"He'll suspend your ass."

"He's already tried that. But I don't think he would anyway; the Feds would be all over him. They need me. As long as I've got the truth rattling around in my head somewhere, I'm a valuable commodity. But either way, I'm doing what I'm doing. You can help, or not."

"Where would we start?"

"I'm not sure, but first I need to know more about Bennett. Can I get a copy of the file we keep on him?"

"You got a truck to transport it? I'll see what I can do."

"Good. Thanks. Are you in or out, Nate?"

Nate thought about it for a while and finally said, "I'm in." He stood up. "But first I need another donut."

"STARTING TONIGHT, I'M STAYING IN MY OWN *apartment."*

"Why?" Nate asks.

"Well, for one thing, you are far too big of a pain in the ass for me to be with you twenty-four/seven. Eight hours a day is more than enough."

He nods. "That's what my girlfriend said before she dumped me."

"You had a serious girlfriend?" I ask, showing more surprise than I should.

"Yeah, actually you liked her. Problem was she didn't like me. She was like a hundred pounds; I outweighed her by two people. What are your other reasons?"

"The doctor said it's more likely that I'll get my memory back if I return to normal, and normal is living in my own home. And I feel strong enough to handle things myself."

"Okay, you're calling the shots," Nate says. "But I'm stationing a black-and-white in front of the building."

"No. I can protect myself."

It has taken a while, but Nate realizes where this is going. "You want them to come after you, don't you? You think you can nail them that way."

"That's the preferred outcome, yes."

"Come on, Doug, you think Bennett is going to come himself? He'll send a soldier twelve rungs down below. And if that guy doesn't do the job, he'll send two others even lower."

"I've got to start somewhere."

About an hour later, Nate drives me to his place and we get my stuff. As promised, he also has two boxes of documents that represent the department's so far unsuccessful efforts to nail Bennett. He then takes me back to my apartment, and on the way I ask, "Hey, where's my car?"

"They took it from the scene and brought it back to your place."

"What kind is it?"

"I told you . . . it's a Crown Vic . . . just like this one. It's department issue."

"What happened to my Mustang?" I gird myself for the answer; I loved that car, it's a classic, and I can't believe I would ever have given it up.

"You still have it; you store it in some garage so nothing can happen to it. You never shut up about it."

When we get to my apartment, I notice that there's a police car sitting in front, with two cops in it. "I told you I don't want them here," I say.

"Tough shit. You're not getting your way on this one."

This is a battle I can afford to lose, so I just nod and take my stuff out of the car. I carry the two bags myself, but I can tell in doing so that I don't nearly have my full strength back. Nate helps carry the boxes of the Bennett documents in, and when we're done I walk him back down to his car.

"Thanks for everything, pal," I say. "I mean it. I know this hasn't been fun for you."

"No sweat. Call me if you need anything, at any time."

"I will."

I go back into the building and get on the elevator, and a young woman gets on with me. "Doug, good to have you back."

I smile. "Thanks, good to be back."

"How is Jessie?"

"Fine. She's fine." I guess Jessie was here a lot; it's starting to look like we weren't just casually dating.

We reach the fourth floor, and the door opens. I hesitate, because I have no idea if she is getting off at this floor as well. She doesn't, and looks at me a little strangely, as if I should know that. I should, Miss Whatever Your Name Is, but I don't, so what do you think of that? "Have a good evening," I say as I get off.

Entering my apartment feels just as strange as it did the other day. There's a sense you get when you're home, a certain level of comfort, and I'm just not feeling it. I'm a visitor here.

I spend the first few minutes throwing out everything in my refrigerator, since it's all expired. Fortunately, there are takeout menus in the kitchen, so I order a pizza, which shows up in a half hour, and costs twice as much as I would have expected. The delivery guy knows me by name; I've got a feeling I don't cook much.

I open up the first box of Bennett documents, and before long I'm immersed in the department's efforts to nail the son of a bitch. Dan Congers and Jerry Bettis took the lead on it a number of years ago, and then I became the unofficial leader. Apparently Congers was partners with Bettis, who I remembered being in the Academy with.

We've obviously not had any success in putting him away, but we have damaged his business. The goal has been to cut off his access to funds, and some success has been achieved. Bennett has a very large, very expensive operation, and we've gotten decent results damaging the financial end of it.

The files are helpful, but I of course wonder what I knew that I didn't put in the file. I can't find anything in the apartment to tip me off. I'd never been much of a note taker, but I was hoping that I had picked it up over the years. If I have, I must also be a good note hider, because I can't locate any.

I see that I have what looks like a fairly new computer, and I start to play around with it. It's called a MacBook Air, and it's really thin. I always used a Mac, so it should be pretty easy.

It should be, but it isn't, and I run into an immediate brick wall. It asks me for my password, and of course I have no idea what that might be. I try some of the ones I think I used in the "old days," but the image on the monitor moves back and forth, left and right, as if it's shaking its head no at me.

I call Nate, and he answers the phone with, "You miss me already?"

"I'm dealing with it," I say. "You have any idea what my computer password is?"

"We were partners, Doug. We weren't married."

I'm feeling frustrated. "I can't even get into my goddamn computer."

"You could call Jessie. She could get in; she's a genius with stuff like that. She might even know it anyway."

"Never mind; I'll keep trying."

I get off the phone and start to look around. There's a small desk in my bedroom, and when I open the drawer there it is, a list of all my passwords. It's probably a terrible idea to keep a record like that, but it sure has worked for me this time.

My password for the computer is "Jessie," and that's also my password for a bunch of Web sites. Sometimes it's "Jessie1," or "Jessie#," or various other versions of "Jessie." I've got a hunch I knew Jessie pretty well.

I don't really know where to begin on the computer, so I just start browsing through it. Most of the bookmarked sites are related to sports in some way, and I start updating myself on what's gone on over the years. There were the two Giant Super Bowl wins, but they didn't do much in the other years. As far as my Mets and Knicks are concerned, it seems to have been a lost decade.

Three-quarters of the way down the list of bookmarks is Mapquest. I go on there, looking to see if it saves the destinations I've used it for in the past, as maybe that could give me some kind of clue. I'm a bit desperate here.

It doesn't save the stuff, or if it does, I can't find it. I wonder if I've even been using Mapquest anymore, or if anyone does, since GPS systems seem so widely used. Even Nate had one in his car, and he was always about as technologically backwards as a person could be. Maybe that's changed.

Something Nate said the other day pops into my mind. I meant to ask him about it, but we were in the middle of a meeting, and afterwards I had forgotten.

I call Nate, and this time he answers the phone with, "Long time, no talk."

"I just love the sound of your voice," I say. "But while I have you . . . the other day you said that when I called you, you asked Jessie to trace the GPS on my phone."

"Right."

"What does that mean?"

"There's a GPS in every phone. The phone company computer can tell where it is all the time, as long as it has cell service. Big Brother is everywhere these days."

"Does it keep a record of where it's been in the past?" I ask.

"Yes. Why?"

"Nate, I was on to something with Bennett; I wouldn't have made that call to you if I wasn't. So I want to retrace my steps, but I don't know what those steps were. Maybe this way we can retrace my phone's steps. That's almost as good."

Nate doesn't say anything for a few moments, and then, "That fall on your head might have smartened you up some. You want to call Jessie and get her started on it?"

"I don't think that's a great idea," I say. "She didn't seem too comfortable around me. You'd know better than me, but I don't think our personal relationship ended too well."

"You guys made a great couple, and then you didn't," Nate said. "I'll call her."

FOR TAHIR SADRI, THE EXCITEMENT WAS WEARING OFF. He had been stuck in that apartment for six weeks, waiting for a call that never seemed to come. When they had contacted him originally it had felt like an honor, like he had been singled out because he was special. It was a recognition of his dedication, and his courage, and his commitment.

He was quite literally the chosen one.

But it had gone on so long. They had told him it might, but he still had a fear that they had forgotten him. Maybe they had switched to someone else, someone they had more confidence in. And maybe that caused them to leave him in that apartment, run by that asshole manager, who watched him like a hawk whenever he came and went. When this was over, before he left town, his plan was to come back and kill that manager. That would be the icing on the cake.

He wasn't positive exactly what his assignment was going to be; the target wasn't identified yet. Or if it had been, it hadn't been shared with him. But he was certain that it would stun the world. He hoped that many Americans would die, and that they would get the message that no one was safe. But that would depend on what he was called upon to do. Whatever it would be, he would be up to the task.

But while Sadri was a loyal soldier, he was not a robot. He had a mind of his own, and he had already decided to make one change in whatever plan they had for him. He knew they saw him as a martyr, and while there was unquestionable glory in that, there was more glory in surviving, then living to strike again, and again.

But for now Sadri could only sit and wait. He knew that someday this wasted time would be of no significance, and would be forgotten. At some point they would contact him, and tell him what he was to do, and most importantly, give him the materials to do it. He had tried to secure them himself, but they had reprimanded him for doing so.

Sadri knew that when that call finally came, he would feel the surge of excitement that he longed for.

His time was coming.

He would be ready.

THE MEETING WITH JESSIE WAS SET FOR 11 A.M.

It was in the conference room of the "cyber section," where she worked. When Doug arrived, she was already there, hunched over a computer. Nate had not arrived yet.

"Good morning," Doug said.

"Hello," she said without looking up.

Doug could hear either tension, or nervousness, or disdain in her voice. He was never great before the shooting at understanding women, and the trauma didn't seem to have advanced that talent any.

He sat down across the table from her and let an uncomfortable two minutes go by before speaking. "I know this is a little awkward for both of us," he said. "Nate told me we went out, and I've seen pictures of you in my apartment."

She hesitated, and then nodded. "We did, but then we stopped."

"I don't know what happened," he said. "But I'm sorry if I did anything wrong or stupid."

"Let's leave it in the past," she said, just as the door opened and Nate came into the room.

"Sorry I'm late," he said, and then saw their faces and felt the tension in the room. "Very sorry I'm late."

"Let's get started," Jessie said in a businesslike tone. She pointed to a large monitor in front of her, and Doug and Nate peered over her shoulders. "Most of this is self-explanatory. Here's the date, time, and duration, and these are the coordinates where the phone GPS registered. I've just started assigning addresses to the coordinates, and I should be finished by the end of the day. The addresses won't necessarily be totally accurate; for example, it could be the house next door to the one I give you."

"I always carried my phone, right?" Doug asked. "I mean, based on my habits, can we assume that wherever the phone was, I was in that place as well?"

"Yeah, definitely," Nate said. "No question."

Doug stared intently at the screen. "Looks like there are three places I spent a lot of time in." He pointed. "Do you know where that is?"

"It's in Hackensack; your apartment."

"What about that one?" he asked.

"That's right here. It's where we are now."

He pointed again. "And that one?"

A beat, and then Jessie said, "That's my house."

Nobody knew what to say, so after a few moments, Nate came up with, "Okay, moving right along, can you give us the first page or two with locations? That way we can get started."

Jessie nodded. "Sure, and I'll get the rest of it done today."

"Thanks, Jess," Nate said, and he and Doug left.

Once they were outside the closed door, Doug said, "She hates me; did I cheat on her?"

"She doesn't hate you, and if you cheated on her, you didn't tell me about it. Which is just as well, because then I would have shot you myself. She's a terrific lady; way too good for you. She deserves somebody like me."

The door then opened behind them, and Jessie was there. She looked as if she was going to say something to Doug, but then turned to Nate, and handed him a piece of paper. "Here, you forgot this; it's page one. It can get you started."

Nate took it as she closed the door behind her. He handed it to Doug, who looked at it quickly and said, "Let's start at the top."

The top, which meant the first place that neither Doug nor Nate could identify, was on Vernon Avenue in Paterson. The house number on Jessie's list was 308, and that's the one Nate ran through the computer. The result was promising: the owner of the house was listed as Bruce Andrus, who a year ago finished a three-year prison term for grand larceny. Andrus was a career criminal and had never been choosy about the type of crime to participate in.

They pulled a photo from the database, so they would know what Andrus looked like, and headed for his house. It was a fairly depressed neighborhood, but populated by mostly hard-working, honest people trying to get by. Andrus, according to his rap sheet, was a notable exception.

There were only a few parking spots available on the street, and Nate parked about fifty yards west of the house. As they approached, they saw someone who looked like Andrus walking in the other direction, coming toward them. He saw them as well, and in a matter of seconds, he was no longer walking; he was running down an alley.

Nate and Doug took off in pursuit, but after only a few strides Doug realized he was in no shape to run. He stopped, backed out of the alley, and positioned himself adjacent to the entrance of the next one, hiding behind the front of a house.

Nate continued the chase, but at his size was not about to catch Andrus. Andrus lengthened the distance between them, and then came running up the next alley. When he was only about fifty feet away, Doug stepped out, drew his gun, and pointed it at him.

"Freeze!" he yelled.

Andrus stopped in his tracks, and instantly obeyed when Doug ordered him to raise his hands. "Come on, man, not again," he said in a pleading voice.

Nate came running toward them, although it was more of a stagger. He was gasping for air when he reached them.

"Anybody home in your house?" Doug asked.

"No," Andrus said.

"Then let's go inside."

Nate was still panting heavily. "Any chance you got an oxygen tent in there?"

They went into Andrus's house and walked into what seemed to be the den. Nate instructed him to sit down in a chair, and they both stood nearby, towering over him. They represented an intimidating pair, especially Nate.

Doug spoke first. "When we were outside, you said 'not again.' What did you mean by that?"

"I meant that last time you hassled me, you said you wouldn't be back. Which has turned out to be bullshit."

"What did I hassle you about?"

Andrus was clearly not understanding the line of questioning. "What kind of question is that?"

Nate moved a step closer and said, "You don't judge the questions, okay, asshole? You just answer them."

"Hey, I just didn't understand what he was asking. You want to know what we talked about? Is that it?"

"Yes," Doug said.

"You don't know?"

"Answer the damn question," Nate commanded. "I'm getting tired of telling you."

"You were asking about this guy."

"What guy?"

"I don't know how to pronounce his name. Like Sadri, or something like that."

"Why was I asking about him?" Doug asked.

"Hey, is this some kind of test or something? Why do I have to tell you stuff you already know?"

This time Nate didn't say anything, just took one menacing step toward Andrus. It was more than enough.

"Okay," Andrus said. "This guy, this Sadri, had been trying to get his hands on some explosives. The plastic kind, real powerful. He was throwing around some money, but not nearly enough."

"What was he going to do with it?"

"I don't know; I didn't want to know."

"Did you sell it to him?" Nate asked.

"Me? Look at this rat hole; you think I sold something for a lot of money? Besides, I don't get involved with shit like that. I'm a pacifist. I'm just telling you what I heard. Word gets around."

"How come I was asking you about this?"

Andrus turned to Nate. "Is he kidding?"

Nate ignored the question and asked one of his own. "Where is Sadri?"

"I don't know where he is now, but I can tell you where he was then. Maybe he's still there, maybe not. I don't keep track of him."

"Then tell us."

"A boardinghouse, off Nash Avenue in Clifton."

"The address?"

"It's 348 Marshall Street."

"You sure?" Doug asked.

Nate answered the question. "He's sure." Doug looked over and saw Nate staring at the piece of paper Jessie gave him. "It's next on the list," he said.

It was five minutes after they left, when Andrus could be sure they were gone, that he picked up the phone and dialed a number. "He was just here, this time with a partner," was all that he said, smiling at the knowledge that the phone call would net him five thousand dollars.

Andrus didn't think it worth mentioning that this time Doug seemed more than a little strange.

THE BOARDINGHOUSE WAS ON TWO LEVELS, THREE *apartments on each.*

The hallway leading out from each apartment was outdoors, wrapped around the building, much like at a motel. There were indoor/outdoor carpet runners on them that looked like they were installed during the Truman administration. It had started to rain, and the runners had already gotten mushy.

One of the apartments on the main floor had a plate that said MANAGER on it; he or she obviously lived on the premises.

"Look familiar to you?" Nate asked as they pulled up.

"No, not at all." Doug frowned. "That's a real shocker."

"Okay, well, these are your steps we're retracing. What do we do next?"

"Let's talk to the manager."

They knocked on the manager's apartment door, and Harry Draper came to the door. He appeared to be in his mid-fifties, about five foot six, and at least forty pounds overweight. The sleeveless T-shirt with a tear in it that he wore seemed a style that fit the rest of his appearance, and was in line with the general décor of the building.

Draper took one look at Doug and said, "Oh shit, not again."

"We seem to have hit upon a theme," Nate said.

"What do you want this time?" Draper asked.

"Can we come in? Or do you want to join us in the rain?"

Draper sighed, opened the door, then turned and let them follow him inside. "We want to talk to you about Sadri," Doug said.

Draper frowned. "That's a real fucking news flash."

Doug indicated Nate. "My partner wants to hear directly from you everything you told me last time. Don't leave anything out."

"Directly from me."

"Right. Everything you told me."

"Before or after you threatened to shoot me and toss my body in the ocean if I didn't talk?" Draper asked.

"Before and after. And by the way, the threat still holds."

"Well, I told you that the guy was quiet, didn't talk much to anyone. The only time he didn't shut up was when he was in his apartment. He prayed a lot; you could hear him from the damn street. He was one of those Islam guys."

"Keep going."

"Well, you asked me if he got any visitors, and I said I never saw any. But I don't spend all day watching his apartment, so I can't be sure."

"Do you provide cleaning services in the apartments?" Doug asked.

Draper nodded. "That's what you asked me last time, and I said sure, we have a lady come in twice a week. But he never let her in, told her straight out that he'd clean the place himself. Yeah, I'll bet he did; the place is probably a pigsty."

"Does he pay his rent on time?" Nate asked.

"He did, but I think he may have skipped out on me."

"What makes you say that?"

"I haven't seen him in two days, and he's three days late with the rent. And last weekend he showed up with a suitcase, and brought it into his place."

"An empty suitcase?" Doug asked.

"Do I have X-ray vision?"

"Think about this; picture him carrying it. Did it look like it had some weight to it, by the way he held it?"

Draper took a few moments to actually try and recall it. "Yeah, I think it did."

"Anything else about it that you remember?"

"Yeah. I saw him get to the door to his place, and he reached in his pocket, I think it was the right one, for the key. But it wasn't there, so he reached into the left one and found it."

"So?"

"So he didn't put the suitcase down. He held it the whole time, and just switched it to his other hand when he needed to reach into the other pocket. I remember thinking that was weird, especially because it looked heavy."

Doug said, “We’re going to need to get into that apartment.”

“You got a warrant, or probable cause?” Doug and Nate exchanged glances, prompting Draper to add, “Yeah, I know how this works. I got rights.”

“You do?” Doug asked. “Good for you. When is rent due on these apartments?”

“End of the month. No exceptions, no extensions. My tenants all know that.”

“Or they get evicted?”

Draper nodded. “Damn right. I ain’t running no homeless shelter here.”

“So you just said that Sadri is three days late. Evict his ass and let us into his apartment.”

“I don’t think so,” Draper said.

“Or, I’ve got another idea to run by you; tell me if you like this better,” Nate said. “Instead of wasting time checking out his apartment, we can hang out down here with you and your rights, looking for building code violations. Maybe get some city inspectors to come down. They have rights too.”

Draper frowned and said, “You guys ever lose?”

Nate smiled. “Not so far.”

THE INSIDE OF SADRI'S APARTMENT HAD THAT LIVED-IN *look.*

Dirty dishes in the sink, empty food containers on the kitchen table, an unmade bed, shirts lying on two chairs, and even a small amount of cash on the kitchen counter. Not only did the place have that "lived-in" look, but it had that "still lived-in" look. Sadri's clothing and toiletries were still there; if he left, he hadn't taken his things with him.

"Is this the first time I've been in here?" Doug asked.

"You're asking me if you've been in here?" Draper asked. "How the hell should I know?"

They instituted a quick and reasonably thorough search of the apartment and found nothing significantly incriminating, and certainly no explosives. There was some anti-U.S. literature, but nothing that could be deemed overtly threatening, and clearly no cause to arrest Sadri, if they'd known where he was. One thing that was not there was the suitcase that Draper had seen him bring in.

The item of most interest was a laptop computer with a printer attached to it. "You got wireless in here?" Nate asked.

"What do you think this is, Starbucks?" Draper said.

"I'm getting a little tired of your mouth," Nate said. "How many teeth did you have when the day started?"

"Sometimes you can pick up the signal from the Dunkin Donuts across the street. But it's pretty weak."

Doug sat down, turned it on, and was immediately greeted by the request for a password. "Here we go again," he said, and then turned to Draper. "What do you do with the personal belongings of people you've evicted?" Doug asked.

"Whatever I want. I own it. But it's never worth much, or the people who owned it wouldn't have been living here in the first place."

"Good. Then you're telling us that this is now your computer. We're going to borrow it."

"Keep it. Just leave me alone and don't come back, okay?"

Nate handed him his card. "Be a good citizen; call me if Sadri shows his face."

Doug and Nate left with Sadri's computer and headed back to the barracks. "This another job for Jessie?" Doug asked.

"Yeah."

"Is this cyber stuff all she does?"

Nate nodded. "Yeah, it is now, and she's not too happy about it. She used to be in a car, and was a damn good cop. Then she took some tech courses that the department offered, sort of as an extra thing. She was great at it, and then the whole cybercrime area exploded, so now she's doing it full time. She misses the action."

"You ever going to tell me what happened between me and her?"

"Not me; none of my business."

"Come on, Nate. She hates me, and I want to know why."

Nate thought about it for a few moments, and then said, "Let's put it this way . . . you're an asshole."

"You've got a real way with words."

"We need to bring the task force into this," Nate said, referring to the Joint Terrorism Task Force, and changing the subject.

Doug shook his head. "Too soon. What the hell have we got? One loser said another loser was looking for explosives. We have no evidence that he got any, or what he would do with them if he did."

"I know what's going on; you want to do this on your own."

Doug nodded. "For the second damn time."

"The doc was right; you haven't changed at all," Nate said. "Sorry, but I've at least got to bring Congers into the loop. He works for us, assigned to the task force. We can't go it alone on this, Doug. If we do, and Sadri blows up a building, with some people in it . . ."

"Okay. I get it."

"When we get back, you take the computer to Jessie, and I'll call Congers."

That is what they did, but Jessie was out for lunch, and was due back in twenty minutes. Doug took a seat outside her office to wait for her.

Nate, meanwhile, went to his own office and called Congers. He explained the situation about Sadri, and Congers asked, "You got a first name for this guy?"

"No, just the name Sadri, and the address I gave you."

"No photo? Or prints?"

"No photo, but I can give you an address where you can get all the prints you want. But can't you run it off the name?"

"Probably, but for all I know Sadri is like Smith or Jones."

Nate gave him the address, and then considered telling him about the computer, but decided to give Jessie a shot at it first. "Based on the literature in his apartment, the guy is pretty far out there, hates this country, and we have a witness that says he has been out looking for explosives. Wouldn't you guys have been watching him already?"

"Hey, don't look at me, I just work here. I'll run this down and see what I come up with. Which brings me to the key question: what the hell are you doing with this?"

"Doug and I sort of stumbled on it."

"Yeah," said Congers, clearly not buying it. "Just be careful with this kind of stuff, or you could stumble big time."

"Ah, words of wisdom," Nate said. "I remember when you weren't such hot shit."

"That was long ago, my friend," Congers said. "Long ago."

Once off the call, Nate was about to meet up with Doug in Jessie's office, when Captain Bradley came in and closed the door. "Where the hell have you guys been?" he asked.

"Out policing . . . making you proud . . . making this a safer state for the citizens of New Jersey."

"Don't screw with me, Nate, or you'll be working a grammar school crossing with a defective whistle. Now what are you doing?"

"Doug's retracing his steps, and I'm helping him, and trying to keep him from getting shot again."

"I told you, and I told him, regular duty. Was I not clear about that?"

"You were clear, Captain. But with all due respect, he doesn't really give a shit; he's going to do what he wants to do. And he doesn't much care if you suspend him; he's still going to do it. So I figured he should do it in house, where we can watch him."

"That is not acceptable."

"He doesn't think it's acceptable to have someone out there who put two bullets into his body, without trying to find that person. So that's what he's doing."

JESSIE COMES TOWARD HER OFFICE AND SEEMS *surprised to see me sitting here.*

It's clear that I make her nervous, but not in a good way; more in a very uncomfortable, get him the hell out of here soon way.

There is something familiar about her; I can't place it, but I felt it the first time I saw her. Or at least the first time I remember seeing her. She is the only person or thing that seems to jog my memory in any way. I can't recall anything about knowing her before I was shot, but I have this vague feeling that the memories are there somewhere.

I'm definitely attracted to her. Nate said that I was an asshole when it came to our relationship, which must mean on some level that I pushed her away. At this point it's hard to imagine why I would have done that.

"Hi," I say. My injuries have obviously made me quite the conversationalist.

"I didn't realize you were waiting for me. Do you

need something?" Then she sees the computer in my hand. "Need a little help with that?"

"More than a little."

"Come on in."

We go into her office; I see that she has a lot of pictures on the wall and on her desk, none of which include me. She starts setting up the computer at her workstation. The silence is getting on my nerves a bit, so I say, "Nate said you're great at this stuff, but that you'd rather be out on the street, like before."

"Did he now," she says, more of a statement than a question.

"He said you miss the action, and that you're a really good cop."

"You and Nate seem to talk about me a lot." She is not looking up from what she's doing as she responds.

"He talks. I listen, because I have nothing to add."

"Uh-huh," she says.

Once again I can tell I'm making her uncomfortable, without really knowing why. I probably should just shut up, but I can't seem to. "You mind my talking to you like this? I don't mean any harm, and definitely don't want to pry. I'm just trying to get to know you."

This seems to touch a nerve, because for the first time she turns away from what she's doing and looks me straight in the eyes. "Doug, you know me better than anyone in the world. You know me better than I know me. You just don't remember any of it. And you know what? It's probably better that way, so I'm not about to reeducate you. Let's leave it where it is."

"Nate said that when it came to you, I was an asshole."

"You were not an asshole. Nate is an asshole."

"Asshole Nate reporting for duty," he says as he walks in, obviously having heard what Jessie said. "I love when people talk about me."

"I don't," she says. "Can we wrap up the *Days of Our Lives* episode and get to the computer? Tell me what you need."

"It belongs to a potential suspect who seems to have disappeared. We need to get into that computer, and see if it contains anything that would lead us to an understanding of his actions, and especially his whereabouts."

"What kind of actions do you suspect him of?" she asks.

"Terrorism of some kind, target unknown," I say. "We do know he has been trying to get explosives; we don't know if he's managed to do so."

"So this is a priority."

I nod. "This is very definitely a priority."

She plugs the computer into a power source and turns it on. Then she starts to press some keys, stops, and presses some more. Then she goes through that process again. I have absolutely no idea what she's doing, but I'm pretty sure she does.

After about five minutes of this, she says, "This is going to take a while."

"Call one of us when it's ready, okay?"

"I will."

With nothing to do but wait, we go back to Nate's office. Nate brings me up to date on his conversation with the captain. “Bradley’s pissed,” he says. “He gave us an order, and we ignored it.”

“I don’t give a shit.”

“I mentioned that to him,” Nate says. “He didn’t take it that well. I think it has something to do with him being captain, and you not being captain.”

“He didn’t get shot,” I point out.

“I didn’t either.”

“Hey, Nate, I’m not asking you to do anything you’re not comfortable with. I told you that from the beginning. If you want out, I understand.”

“I get that,” he says. “But we don’t want to get our asses suspended. We’ve got a much better chance to do what we need to do with the resources of the department behind us.”

I understand he’s right about that, so I say, “So keep him pacified.”

He laughs a short laugh. “Boy, you really don’t remember him.”

“I’m concerned we’re getting off the track,” I say. “This thing with Sadri doesn’t feel like it has a connection to Bennett. From what I’ve read, and what you’ve told me, it doesn’t feel like his style.”

“I agree,” Nate says. “But it does fit better with Gharsi, the guy whose picture you sent me. And he doesn’t seem to have a connection to Bennett either, at least not that we know of.”

“Is it possible it wasn’t Bennett I was after? I didn’t actually mention his name in the phone call.”

“I don’t think so,” Nate says. “You were on suspension, and nothing about either Sadri or Gharsi was on our radar before you left. How would you have come to be after them? It was Bennett you were after. When you said 'I got him,' that has to be who you were talking about."

We talk about it some more, not getting anywhere. Congers calls back to tell Nate that in fact Sadri is in the task force database, but was not considered a significant risk. "That doesn't mean he isn't," Congers says. "He's certainly not a choirboy. Keep me posted on whatever you learn." Congers has also electronically transmitted photographs of Sadri, and both Nate and I look at them carefully.

After that, I stand up and tell Nate, "I'm out of here."

"You want to grab something to eat?"

"No. I want to get home, turn on my computer, and study more about the world. So far I'm not impressed by the progress in the last ten years. By the way, I got an e-mail yesterday telling me that some woman I don't know wants to 'friend' me. What the hell does that mean?"

"It means she wants to sleep with you."

"That's what they call it now?"

"Yup."

"So what do I do?" I ask.

"You don't remember what you do when a woman wants to sleep with you? This is worse than I thought."

"Never mind."

"I'll be at the Blazer if you're looking for me," he says.

"What is the Blazer?"

He shakes his head. "Man, you have a lot to catch

up on. It's the sports bar we go to maybe four times a week. You remember what beer is?"

"Vaguely."

"By the way, I bought last time, so next time we go, you get the check."

"DOUG? IT'S JESSIE."

I would be surprised and pleased that she has called me at home, but I can hear the stress in her voice. "What's going on?"

"I can't reach Nate, he's not answering his phone, and—"

"He's at a sports bar . . . it's called the Blazer. Maybe he doesn't hear the phone. Is it something you can tell me?"

"I went through this guy Sadri's computer. He's a fanatic; he's been on every terrorist Web site you can imagine. And searching all kinds of things about explosives."

"I'm not surprised. I'll come in with Nate tomorrow and we can go over it."

"No," she says quickly. "There's something else; something that I don't think can wait."

"What?"

"He bought and printed out an advance ticket for a

movie. It's an eight o'clock showing tonight of *The End of Time*."

I've seen TV ads for it; it looks like one of those summer blockbusters. This is very worrisome: I just can't buy that Sadri is taking time out of his terrorist day to take in a movie. "Where is it playing?"

"The Martin Ten-plex," she says.

"Where is that?"

"What? We've been there a million—" She catches herself, having forgotten in the moment that I'm operating on a ten-year tape delay. "It's in the Bergen Mall in Paramus. Do you know where that is?"

"Yes. Jessie, please call the Blazer, get Nate to the phone, tell him what's going on, and have him meet me at the theater. Then get a hold of Congers and tell him the same thing. Make sure they understand it's urgent."

"Will do."

"Thanks," I say, grabbing my car keys as I hang up the phone. It's seven twenty, and the drive to the theater will take about fifteen minutes. I have no idea where the Blazer is, so I don't know when Nate will arrive. By the time Jessie is able to reach Congers and brief him, it will likely be too late for him to intervene.

So it's on me.

I head for the car, trying to summon to mind the photos that Congers had sent of Sadri. That theater is likely to be packed, and it's not going to be easy to pick him out. Fortunately my ability to create new memories hasn't been affected, and I've always been pretty good with faces.

Like with everything else, my last recollection of night traffic on these roads is ten years old, so I don't know what I am going to encounter. Unless I have a fairly quick trip, then I've got to just hope that in addition to being a fanatic terrorist, Sadri is also a movie buff.

I'm in luck; there isn't much traffic at all. My luck further holds when I remember the complex turns that will get me to the mall; that doesn't seem to have changed over the years. I check my watch when I get to the theater parking lot, and it's twenty-five to eight.

I leave the car near the front of the theater, parking in a handicap spot. I do so carefully and without screeching my brakes; I don't want Sadri to see me and get spooked by anything I might do.

I run toward the theater and am shocked to see Nate coming this way as well. Obviously the Blazer is near here. "You see him?" he asks, when he reaches me.

"No."

He looks up at the marquee. "The eight o'clock show is in theater four. Let's go."

We show our badges to the elderly gentleman taking tickets, and move into the huge lobby. We both scan the area for Sadri. "I don't see him," Nate says. "I'm going to go into the theater."

"Nate, hold it a second," I say, and point ahead and to the right. "Could that be him?" I can only see the man from a side angle; it's not a great one, but it could be Sadri. He's wearing a fairly large backpack strapped over his shoulders. It hangs as if it is heavy.

"Only one way to find out," Nate says, and he immediately starts moving toward the man.

"Wait," I say, although I'm not sure why, since I don't have a better plan. In any event, Nate is not listening to me, and he is already bearing down on the unsuspecting backpack carrier. All I can do is move toward them as well, while also trying to check out the room, in case it's not Sadri that Nate is going after.

I see Nate reach the man and put his hand on his shoulder, turning him. The man reacts, but I can't tell if it's an aggressive move, or if he's just surprised at being grabbed in this manner. I'm frozen in place, watching this play out.

There seems to be a small struggle, or at least increased movement, and suddenly I hear the unmistakable sound of a handgun round being fired. Nate's legs look like they buckle slightly, and then he slumps slowly to the ground. Everybody in the lobby turns toward the noise, though they don't know the origin yet.

The man I now know is definitely Sadri doesn't even watch Nate fall; he looks around the room quickly and then starts to move toward the theater. There is no way I can let him do that; I'm positive his backpack is filled with explosives, and he's got a gun.

I go to draw my own gun and see that it is already in my hand; my instincts must have taken over. "Sadri! Freeze!"

He turns quickly, without stopping, but I don't think he sees me. Then he speeds his pace, but there are a few other patrons blocking his path. He pushes them out of the way. One thing he doesn't do is freeze.

Firing in this crowded lobby is insane, especially as people are starting to run around in panic, not really knowing where the danger or shooting is coming from. But the disaster will become far greater if Sadri gets into that theater.

I wait a brief second, and then get as good a look as I'm going to get. I fire off one round, and Sadri's head explodes as if it were a melon. By this point, frightened, screaming people are leaving the theater in droves, nearly running me over in the process. It's all I can do to make it to Nate, who is on his back and bleeding heavily from his abdomen.

I rip off my shirt and press it on the wound as hard as I can. If Nate isn't unconscious, he's close to it; he certainly isn't responding to me. I'm pretty sure he's alive.

"CALL AN AMBULANCE!" I scream, hoping someone out of all these people will actually do it. "CALL A GODDAMN AMBULANCE!"

CALVIN WINKLER WAS ANNOYED.

He should have been able to leave work three hours earlier, but instead he was stuck in his office at the executive airport in Millerton, New Jersey. And it was all because of one plane that had arrived for the first time at the airport three days earlier, and was just scheduled to leave this night.

So Calvin had been forced to cancel a date, and it wasn't like he had so many of them to cancel. The woman had been pissed off; that was clear from her voice. Calvin was not the type to get away with canceling dates two hours before he was supposed to pick the woman up. It had taken him three months to get her to say yes in the first place, and when he called it off, she certainly had not mentioned anything about a rain check.

So the six-seater jet was fueled and ready on the tarmac, and Calvin was impatiently waiting for the owner to show up and take off, so Calvin could get the hell out of there. It's not like he was paid for overtime; he wasn't even paid enough for regular time.

From his vantage point in the office, it was not possible for him to see the two cars stop just outside the airport grounds. Nor did he see one man, Aakif Malek, quickly get out of his car and get into the passenger seat of the car driven by Ahmat Gharsi.

Malek did not know why Gharsi was leaving Malek's car outside the grounds, but he was not about to question him. Gharsi was a near-God in his eyes, and whatever his plan was, Malek would do whatever was necessary. He was thankful that he had gone for the pilot training as they had instructed, and knew that was the reason he had been chosen for this assignment.

Malek would, if truth be told, willingly give his life for Gharsi.

They pulled into the airport parking lot, and Gharsi shut off the car. "It is waiting out there," Gharsi said. "I will see you shortly."

They got out of the car, and Gharsi went into the very small terminal building. Malek, as he had been instructed, waited alongside the car until he heard what would be the signal.

Gharsi walked into the building, seeming to shield his face with his hands, though knowing full well he was doing so ineffectively, and that the surveillance cameras would enable him to be identified.

He saw Winkler sitting at the desk. "There you are," Winkler said, leaving off the words he wanted to say, which were, "It's about time." If this guy had a plane, that meant he was rich, and if there was one thing Winkler knew for sure, it's that it's never a good idea to piss off rich people.

Had Winkler uttered those words, they would have been the last he ever spoke. Gharsi smiled but didn't bother to answer; he simply took out his handgun and put a bullet in Winkler's forehead.

He then went into the office, located the control panel for the surveillance cameras, and shut them off. Secure in the knowledge that he could no longer be watched, he walked out of the building and toward the waiting plane.

Malek heard the expected gunshot and, as previously instructed, walked around the building and met Gharsi at the plane. He carried with him the locked suitcase that had been in Gharsi's car.

Gharsi took the suitcase from him and loaded it onto the plane, handling it carefully. Malek had no idea what was in it, but was sure it must be valuable. He would make certain it got to its destination safely.

"Do you have any questions?" Gharsi asked.

"No. I have committed the plan to memory," he said. It wasn't all that complicated; he was to fly to a similar airport in New Brunswick, Canada, where people loyal to the cause would be waiting for him. They would then load the suitcase on a jet to fly back to the homeland, and provide Malek with transportation home. There he would await further instructions, and additional assignments.

Malek boarded the Cessna 5 and pulled the door shut. He waited until Gharsi had walked clear of the plane, and then taxied out onto the runway. Gharsi walked back around the side of the terminal and then toward the car that Malek had left off the airport grounds.

He never bothered to turn and watch the plane's departure.

Malek's takeoff was smooth; he was more than capable of handling the aircraft, and within minutes he was out over the ocean and heading toward New Brunswick. He had brought the suitcase into the cockpit alongside him, so he could make sure it wasn't jostled and damaged if they hit any turbulence.

The suitcase was still sitting there when it exploded, sending the dead Malek and the pieces of the shattered plane into the Atlantic.

By then Gharsi was driving toward the city, way too far away to hear or see the blast.

But he was smiling; the preliminary round had gone perfectly.

And the main event was still to come.

IT SEEMED AS IF THE ENTIRE WORLD DESCENDED ON *the theater.*

Three separate law enforcement agencies were on the scene: the local Paramus cops, New Jersey State Police, and members of the Joint Terrorism Task Force. Congers had called in the latter; they were there in force, and they were in control.

A fleet of ambulances arrived within minutes. It was unclear how many casualties there were; the call that came in simply talked about a shooting in a crowded theater. Just based on previous, similar incidents, it seemed prudent to assume a large number of wounded, and hospitals had been alerted to be ready. They would find that Nate was the only shooting victim requiring care; there were eleven other injuries, mostly minor, from people being injured in the mad race to flee the theater.

All Sadri needed was a body bag.

The media was also arriving in large numbers. Since the news event was so close to New York City, they were able to get many reporters and camera crews there quickly, local and national. Within minutes, field reporters were standing and talking to cameras, with the theater behind them as a backdrop.

Captain Bradley was there, as was Jessie and just about every one of Nate's fellow officers. Initially it wasn't easy for anyone to get into the theater, because they had to navigate the hundreds of moviegoers fleeing the place.

Doug was only dimly aware of the surroundings; he was focused on Nate's wound, and trying to continue to stem the flow of blood. But when he saw the first police arrive, he had the presence of mind to warn them that there were very likely explosives in the fallen Sadri's backpack.

This news caused everyone other than EMS workers and a few agents to clear the lobby. Doug reluctantly left Nate in the care of the medics, and went out to the parking lot. He felt lost, alone among all those people.

"Doug, what happened in there?"

He turned and saw that it was Jessie, and Bradley was coming up toward them as well.

"Nate was shot," he said. "I think it's bad."

"Who did it?" Bradley asked.

"His name is Sadri . . . was Sadri . . . he's dead. He was going to blow up the theater. Nate stopped him."

Just then the EMS people came out of the theater, wheeling Nate on a gurney, heading for the ambulance. Bradley ran over and talked to them as they loaded Nate into the vehicle. He came back to Doug and Jessie as the ambulance pulled away.

"He's alive, but vital signs are weak. They won't know how bad it is until they get him to the hospital."

"I'm going there," Doug said.

Bradley shook his head. "No, you're going to have to be debriefed and give a statement on what happened here tonight."

"To whom?"

"The Feds. They're already coming down on this with both feet."

Doug looked around and was surprised to see that the parking lot had emptied quickly. Officers were setting up a perimeter at least three hundred yards from the theater, no doubt in deference to the presumed presence of explosives. In the distance, Doug could see that Route 4 was already clogged in both directions with bumper-to-bumper traffic. He hoped it didn't seriously impede the ability of Nate's ambulance to get him to the hospital as quickly as possible.

All things considered, the evacuation was going in a fairly orderly fashion. The only people offering any resistance at all were the media members, but when they learned about the nature of the danger, they moved along rather quickly. No sense getting blown up on national TV; that was not part of the job description. They wanted to live to broadcast another day.

Three bomb squad unit vans pulled up to the front of the theater, and the officers headed inside. That was one job in law enforcement that Doug had never envied, or at least not that he could remember.

Congers came over to them and said, "Captain, you

and Jessie have to move behind the perimeter. They're going to be examining the device and then bringing it out." He indicated Doug. "And I'm going to need our boy here."

"Where are we going?"

"The Bureau. And you're going to talk, and talk, and talk some more."

WILSON METCALF, FBI AGENT IN CHARGE, CONDUCTED *Doug's interview.*

More accurately, he conducted the final interview, after Doug had repeatedly told the entire story to two other agents in consecutive sessions. Congers had been present for both of those sessions, but this was just Metcalf and Doug.

Doug had briefly noticed Metcalf at the theater before departing, so he figured that if Metcalf was here now, things must have been wrapped up there.

It was almost past midnight when they started. "You've had quite a night," Metcalf said.

"Yeah."

"Where'd you learn to shoot like that?"

"Shooting school," Doug said, his annoyance showing. "Look, we're not going to chitchat, are we? I'm tired and I've told everybody everything. Twice. How is Nate?"

"I got a report about a half hour ago. Critical but stable; whatever the hell that means."

"What was in Sadri's backpack?"

"Enough explosives to level the entire mall."

"So when can I get out of here?" Doug asked.

"I'm your last stop," Metcalf said, and then proceeded to ask mostly the same questions that Doug had already answered repeatedly. Then he asked, "So, just to be clear, since you were released from the hospital, you have had no additional contact with, or information about, Ahmat Gharsi?"

"No. Was Gharsi behind this?"

Metcalf paused for a moment, then said, "We have information that Gharsi commandeered a plane tonight, which blew up over the Atlantic Ocean."

"So he's dead? You're sure?"

Metcalf nodded. "As sure as we can be where Gharsi is concerned. He murdered an airport worker and then disabled the cameras, but we have him on tape just before that."

"So Gharsi was behind Sadri?"

"I think that's a fair assumption; I would be very surprised to learn otherwise."

"Who blew up his plane?"

"Probably no one. More likely he had explosives with him that detonated, maybe from pressure in the cabin. But again, no way to be sure; he certainly wasn't communicating with air traffic control."

"And Bennett?" Doug asked. "Does he fit in to this?"

"This will go quicker if I ask the questions," Metcalf said. "Have you gotten any of your memory back?"

Doug shook his head. "No. Nothing. What about Bennett?"

"My best guess is that you were investigating something else, maybe Bennett, maybe not, and you stumbled on Gharsi. You made a mistake, and you got shot. But you retraced your steps, and had a do-over tonight. And you won."

"So you don't think Bennett is connected to tonight?" Doug asked again.

"Bennett's name does not belong in the same sentence as Gharsi or Sadri. They are criminal apples and terrorist oranges."

"I don't feel like I won tonight. Not with Nate . . . ," Doug said, not finishing the sentence.

"The world will think you won," Metcalf said. "By tomorrow morning you'll be a national hero. You'll be on goddamn Wheaties boxes. Millions will breathlessly await your tweets."

"What the hell are my tweets?"

"Never mind; you'll find out."

"Can the hero leave now?"

Metcalf nodded. "Yeah, we know where to find you. I hope your partner is okay."

"Thanks."

I'M TIRED, MAYBE MORE TIRED THAN I'VE EVER BEEN IN *my life.*

Of course, since I don't remember a good portion of my life, I could be wrong about that. But it has been an exhausting day, and the feeling is magnified by the fact that I'm not fully recovered from my injuries. I don't seem to have an extra gear I can kick into.

I can't get Nate out of my mind; he was literally bleeding through my hands, all because he went after Sadri and I didn't. That should have been me; I should have been quicker. I used to act on instinct; that was something I trusted and could fall back on. Maybe my injury has set me back, or maybe I lost the ability years ago. I just don't know.

I wish my memory loss could restart now; I do not want to have to remember tonight.

I turn on the radio, and have to listen to almost ten minutes of the recounting of the events, and my role in them. Metcalf was right—they don't know that much, but they know enough to have already decided that I'm a hero. Nate gets mentioned, but almost as an afterthought, and his condition is said to be unknown.

I decide to go to the hospital, and I see that some of my fellow officers are standing around outside, as if on a vigil. I greet them, though I don't remember most of their names, and they tell me that Nate is on the fifth floor. "Same as you were," one of them says.

I get off the elevator and go to the waiting room, where another four cops are sitting. Jessie is one of them, and when she sees me enter the room, she stands and comes over to me.

"Doug," is all she says, and then puts her head on my chest. I put my arms around her and hold her for at least a minute. It feels good, it feels familiar, and it feels good that it feels familiar.

One of us finally breaks it off, I'm not sure who, and I ask, "How is he?"

"I don't know. He's still in surgery, and they say it'll take at least another hour."

"You want to go down and have some coffee?" I ask.

She smiles, very slightly. "Only if they don't have scotch."

When we get downstairs, she sits at a table and I tell her I'll get the coffee. "How do you take it?" I ask. She smiles, and I ask why.

"Never mind."

"Come on," I say, prodding her.

"Okay. We used to make fun of each other, because I drink it black, with nothing in it, and you take milk and sugar. You'd say we were reversing the male-female roles."

"I take it with milk and sugar? Since when?"

She nods. "For the last couple of years."

"I don't eat broccoli or asparagus, do I?"

"God forbid."

I get the coffees and bring them back to her. We sit without talking for a few moments, and she says, "I can't believe this is happening again."

"What?"

"Sitting in this hospital, worrying, waiting for the doctor to come out of surgery."

"You were here the night I got shot?" I ask.

She nods. "I was. Maybe I'm good luck."

"I'm scared," I say. "He didn't move at all once he went down."

"You want to talk about what happened tonight?"

I shake my head. "Not really; I've already told the story four times, and it never gets any better. Do you mind?"

"No. I'm sure I'll read all about it."

For the first time, at least for the first time that I can remember, it doesn't feel uncomfortable to be with her. More important, I guess, is that she seems more at ease as well.

I proceed to say something that is likely to screw that up. "Since we're not talking about tonight, do you want to talk about what happened between us? That's not something I'll be able to read about."

"No. Do you mind?"

"I hope I didn't do anything to hurt you."

"Let's go upstairs," she says, avoiding the subject. "In case the doctor comes out earlier than expected."

He doesn't come out earlier than expected, and we wait almost two hours before we finally see him. During that time we say very little; Jessie has seemed to withdraw into her protective shell again. Or maybe I'm imagining that, and she's just quiet because she's worried about Nate.

"He's lost a lot of blood, but it could have been much worse," is how the doctor starts the conversation. As conversation starters go, this is a pretty good one, and then he makes it even better. "It will be a long haul back, but unless something unforeseen develops, he should recover fully."

I can see Jessie's legs sag a bit in relief, and I say to her, "You are good luck."

We ask the doctor a few more questions, but we've already gotten the key information. There's no way we can see Nate tonight, and the doctor doubts whether tomorrow will work either. But that's okay; we can wait.

When he leaves, I turn to Jessie. "Can I give you a ride home?"

"No thanks. I have a car."

"Can I walk you to it?"

"Doug, give it time."

THERE ARE ELEVEN MESSAGES ON MY ANSWERING *machine when I get home.*

I listen to the first two, and they're both from media outlets wanting to interview me about tonight's events. I don't bother listening to the rest; I just turn off the ringer.

I'm tired and I want to go to sleep.

I set the alarm for eight o'clock and I sleep until it wakes me. Had I set it for September, I would have slept until it woke me. I get up and turn the phone ringer back on, and it's actually ringing as I do so.

The caller ID says that it's "NJ State Police" calling, so I pick it up. "Doug?" the energetic voice asks. This guy seems like he's been up for a while. "Doug, this is Grant Friedman. I'm the public information officer. We reconnected the other day."

"Reconnected" is an interesting way to put it. "Hello, Grant. What can I do for you?"

"I've been trying to call you, but your message box is full."

I look at the machine, and now it says I have twenty-nine messages, which must be capacity. People must have been calling all night; apparently no one sleeps in 2015. "You got me now," I say.

"As you can imagine, media outlets are falling all over themselves to interview you. We've got requests from everywhere, even international."

"I'm not interested; I haven't done anything worth talking about."

"I appreciate that you feel that way," Grant says. "But the governor feels differently."

He must be kidding. "The governor?" I ask, while realizing that I don't even know who the governor is these days.

"Yes. He's quite proud of you. We all are."

I don't like where this is going. "Thank him for me, so I can go back to sleep."

"Sorry, Doug. But I'm quite sure I speak for the governor when I tell you that the sleep portion of your day just ended. It's the price of fame."

He proceeds to tell me that there are so many outlets, national and local, that want to interview me that it would be clearly impossible to honor all the requests. So the governor and commissioner want me to have one large press conference, to accommodate everyone and get the story out as we want it told.

Left unsaid is the obvious fact that the governor wants it made clear that it was the New Jersey State Police that thwarted this attack, and not the federal government. The same New Jersey State Police that reports in to that same governor, whatever his name is.

As if there was any doubt about that, the press conference is to take place in Trenton, the state capital. It's at two o'clock, and they will send a car to take me down there. Until then I am to stay in my apartment, and not speak to any members of the press.

I don't argue with him, but I have no intention of sitting here all morning. My plan is to go to the hospital and see how Nate is. Unfortunately, I change my plan when I look outside the window and see that what looks like a media mosh pit has formed at the entrance to the building. There's no way I am going to be able to get through that mob without an armed convoy.

I call Jessie at the office, to see if she has any information on Nate. She's not in yet, but they patch me through to her cell phone.

"I'm just leaving the hospital now," she says when I tell her what I want. "They're not letting him have any visitors because he's still in intensive care. But everyone seems pleased at how he's doing."

"Very glad to hear it," I say.

"Are you coming in to the office?"

"Apparently not. They have set up a press conference for me in Trenton."

"I'm not surprised," she says. "They want to show you off."

I get off the phone and grab an hour of additional sleep before getting up to shower and get dressed. Grant Friedman calls me back to tell me that arrangements have been made to take me through the furnace room out to the back of the building, where the car will be waiting.

Even if the media people figure it out, they will be prevented from going back there.

The car turns out to be a limo, and when I get in I see that Friedman and Captain Bradley are in the back waiting for me. They use the time on the way down to Trenton to brief me on what I am to say during the press conference. Basically, it boils down to one word.

Nothing.

I am to say nothing, unless you consider "I'm sorry, I can't speak about that, because it's part of an ongoing investigation" to be something. I can't even answer if they ask me what my favorite cereal is, because for all I know they stopped making Cinnamon Special K five years ago.

This is going to be one hell of a boring press conference.

When we arrive, we're brought into the governor's office. He tells me how proud of me he is, in a tone as if he were my father and I just brought him a terrific report card. Then we all go downstairs to the press room, where the media people are packed in like sardines. They are all talking, and it sounds like a low roar, until we walk in and the place instantly gets quiet.

The governor says what seems like a few thousand words by way of introduction, and I walk to the podium. The reporters start to fire questions at me, about everything from what happened at the theater, to how I knew to be there, to if there are other conspirators, to what was going through my mind as I fired the fatal shot.

I successfully deflect all of them, until they ask me what it feels like to be a hero. "I have no idea," I say. "If I ever become a hero, I'll let you know."

Then someone asks me what Nate's role was in all of this, and I can't help pouncing on it. "He's the real hero," I say. "If it wasn't for him stopping the perpetrator, we'd still be counting the bodies today. Every single person in that theater, including me, owes their life to Nate Alvarez."

I think that my comments about Nate must have been off-script, because Friedman announces that the next question will be the last. I am the designated hero; that doesn't leave much room for Nate.

A young woman gets the opportunity to ask the final question. "Is what happened last night connected to the incident in which you yourself were recently shot? And if so, is this a time when you feel some satisfaction in getting your revenge?"

I shrug off and deflect the question, but it momentarily stuns me into realizing something. The words she said that I'm focused on are "is this a time." Actually, it's only two of those words that I care about.

"This time."

I DRIVE BACK IN THE SAME CAR WITH THE SAME PEOPLE. On the way, Captain Bradley, Friedman, and I discuss where we are in the investigation. Bradley's assessment is that it's basically over—that Sadri and Gharsi were the bad guys, and that they are now history. He seems to think the Feds share his view; at least that's what he got from Congers in their conversation.

"I don't know how you were on to them in the first place," Bradley says. "But I guess it really doesn't matter anymore."

I don't agree with him, but I don't want to say so now. He tells me to take some time off, that I have been through so much and could obviously use the rest. "Maybe getting away from this will help your memory," he says. "You've been under a lot of stress."

We don't get back to my apartment until almost 6 P.M. There is still a contingent of media at the entrance of the building, obviously waiting for me, when we pull up. This time I don't sneak around the back; I just plow my way through them. They throw questions at me, and all I say is, "Guys, I'm sorry. I've done enough talking for today."

I call the hospital but can't get an update on Nate's condition, other than the bland description of him "resting comfortably." He's not being allowed visitors, so I order in a pizza and then spend a couple of hours trying to assess the situation, and also figure out a plan to deal with it.

By the time that is accomplished, I feel exhausted, both physically and mentally. I assume it's because I'm not yet back to full strength, though at this point in my life I really don't know what full strength is. Maybe I've been like this for years.

I look in the contacts section on my computer and find Jessie's home phone number. I call her, and it rings three times without her answering. My guess is she sees my number on caller ID and doesn't want to talk to me, but she fools me and answers on the fourth ring.

"Jessie, it's me, Doug."

"Is Nate okay?" she asks. Concern for Nate is probably why she picked up the phone in the first place.

"As far as I know; that's not why I'm calling."

She doesn't say anything; just waits for me to continue and tell her why, in fact, I am calling. I can picture her cringing as she waits.

"I need your help," I say.

"What kind of help?"

"Everybody thinks this is over . . . except me. I don't think it's close to over."

"I don't either," she says.

Her answer surprises the hell out of me. "Why do you say that?"

"First tell me what kind of help you need."

"Can we meet to talk about it? Maybe tomorrow morning?" I ask.

Another hesitation, then, "I was going to stop at the hospital."

"Me too. Seven o'clock? Breakfast after that?"

She hesitates even longer this time, and then finally says, "Okay."

Once we're off the phone, I really want to go to sleep, but it's only nine thirty. I feel like I need to force my-self to get some endurance, so I resolve to stay up for a couple of hours more.

I surf the Web for a while, with the television on as background noise. I haven't checked out what's been go-ing on in pop culture these last ten years, and figure that this is a good opportunity to do so.

There is no doubt the Kardashian family is every-where, but I can't seem to get Google to tell me why. They're famous enough, but it doesn't appear to have come from acting or singing or anything like that. I think their father was O. J. Simpson's lawyer at one point, but I doubt that explains it. Nobody seems to be broadcasting *Keeping Up with the Dershowitzes.*

There also seems to be some kind of fascination with real housewives in various cities. These shows seem to just hang out with people, but I don't know why these particular people were chosen, or why viewers want to watch them hang out. In any event, I think fake housewives might be more interesting.

I check out movies, and there are quite a few names I recognize. Meryl Streep, Al Pacino, Steven Spielberg, George Clooney, Robert De Niro . . . they've all had staying power. Even Clint Eastwood is still around. But there are many more names I'm not familiar with, which I guess shouldn't surprise me.

The TV commercials are really weird. They've got people selling adult diapers and condoms, and announcers are warning that if some product makes you have an erection that lasts more than four hours, you better get some help.

If four hours is the new standard, the world has truly passed me by.

The serious news is a different story. The Middle East is a mess, and the Israelis and Palestinians hate each other almost as much as the Democrats and Republicans. It's the one area where it seems as if I haven't missed a thing.

After an hour I can't take any more, so I set the alarm and go to sleep. I'm up at six to get dressed quickly and leave. There are only two reporters downstairs; it looks like my fifteen minutes of fame might be wrapping up. That's fine with me.

I'm at the hospital to meet Jessie at seven. We still can't get in to see Nate, but the report is encouraging. His condition has been upgraded from critical to serious, and while they won't come out and say so, my sense is that if he's not out of danger, he's getting there.

"Where do you want to go for breakfast?" I ask Jessie. "I saw that the Coach House is still there," I say, referring to a diner on Route 4 that I passed the other day.

"That's fine," she says, but then I think better of it, telling her that it's a busy place, and if I get recognized I don't want it to turn into a media circus. I want us to have some privacy.

"I know the place," she says, and I follow her to a small café in Elmwood Park called The Cupboard. There are only about eight tables, and three of them are occupied. There's a fireplace on the far wall; this must be a nice, cozy place in the winter.

The woman behind the counter's face lights up when she sees us enter, and she comes around and starts walking toward us.

"Marleigh Fletcher," Jessie whispers to me.

"Doug, it's so good to see you. We were so worried."

She surprises me by giving me a big hug. I never used to be the hugging type, and I don't think that's changed. "Thank you, Marleigh. Nice to be back."

She brings us over to a table in the corner, and pours us some really delicious coffee. We wait for a few minutes, but no one gives us menus, and I say I'll ask for them.

"You haven't seen a menu here in years," Jessie says. "You don't need one."

"Of course not," I say. "Because I have a favorite thing that I always order, and that I have along with my coffee with cream and sugar. And that favorite thing is . . ."

"Chocolate-chip pancakes."

Sure enough, without us ordering, Marleigh soon brings over a large stack of chocolate-chip pancakes for me, and granola for Jessie. After one bite I can tell why I never needed a menu.

"So I guess this was our favorite breakfast place?" I ask, when I stop chewing.

"Doug, I don't think I'm up for a trip down memory lane. What do you need help with?"

"I want you to try and get me shot again."

She thinks about it for a moment and says, "That works for me."

"DID YOU HEAR THE TAPE OF MY PHONE CALL TO NATE, *just before I got shot?"*

Jessie nods. "Maybe fifty times. We were trying to identify other voices, background noise, anything that might help. No luck. Just ambient street noise."

"I only heard it once, but I'm pretty sure I'm right. At one point I said, 'I got him, Nate. This time I got him.' "

"You did. Those were your exact words."

"So it couldn't have been Sadri I was talking about, and it couldn't have been Gharsi. Because I had never gone after them before. I wouldn't have said 'this time' if there hadn't been a previous time."

She shakes her head. "You don't know that, Doug. Maybe you did go after them, and you just don't remember it."

"No, that can't be. Because I was talking to Nate when I said it. I wouldn't have said 'this time' like that unless I thought he would know what I meant. So he would have to have known if I had been after Sadri or Gharsi before, yet at that point he never heard of them."

I can see that she realizes I'm right about this. "So Nate assumed it was Bennett because it was Bennett."

"Exactly; there's no other explanation that I can see. Which means that Bennett and Gharsi were somehow connected."

"That I don't follow," she says.

"I was after Bennett, but I e-mailed Nate a photo of Gharsi. I went to Sadri's apartment, and he was working for Gharsi. Can't be a coincidence; it couldn't be that I was following Bennett and happened to run into an unrelated international terrorist plot. Bennett and Gharsi were working on something together."

"Okay, I buy that."

"Good, now let me try and sell you this. If what I am saying is true, then it's not over. If Gharsi's whole plan was to find a terrorist nut case and blow up a theater, what the hell would he need Bennett for? To take him house-hunting in New Jersey? Maybe the theater was part of it, but there's no way it was everything. It might have just been the opening act; it could even have been a diversion."

"But either way Gharsi is dead," she says.

"That doesn't mean it's over. And even if it is, I'd sort of like to find whoever it was that put a couple of bullets in me, and killed those people at the hotel."

"I understand," she says. "Where do I fit in?"

"Do you have any close contacts in the press? Could be local, could be national; doesn't matter."

She smiles; everybody seems to smile when I say something stupid. "My college roommate is a reporter for *The New York Times*. We went out with her and her husband a bunch of times. You liked her; couldn't stand him."

"No good," I say. "I don't want this traced back to you, and if we use your friend, it will be obvious."

"I'm sure she can set me up with one of her coworkers. What do you want me to say?"

I lay it out for her, and she hates the idea, but she reluctantly agrees to do it when I remind her that if I'm right, then a lot more lives could be on the line. "I'll get on it as soon as I get back to the office."

"Don't call from your office, or even your cell phone," I say. "Use a pay phone."

This time she doesn't smile, she laughs out loud. "A pay phone? It really is like you were dropped here from a different planet."

We get another cup of coffee and talk some more, and I say, "I meant to ask you: last night on the phone, I said this thing with Bennett wasn't close to over, and you agreed. Why did you say that?"

"Because you were intent on getting Bennett. If you had stumbled on something else, you would have turned it over to the rest of the department, and let them handle it. Your entire focus was on Bennett."

"Why?"

"Why was your focus on Bennett?" She knows what I had asked; repeating the question like that is an effort for her to buy time, as she thinks about what she should say.

"Come on, Jessie. You don't want to talk about our dating, or our breakup, I get that. But I'm asking you about something that is clearly an important part of my life, and I have a right to know it. Nobody will be up front with me about it."

She finally nods. "Okay. You coached a baseball team for a few years; the ages of the kids were I think thirteen to fifteen. You loved it, and the kids loved you."

It is beyond weird to hear things in my own life related to me like this, but I don't want to interrupt her to say that. I want her to get where she's going.

"One boy in particular, Johnny Arroyo . . . you were like a father to him. You were great with him, and he worshiped you. His parents had died when he was a little kid, and he went from relative to relative, until he wound up in the foster system. He did not have an easy time of it."

She takes a deep breath, apparently to give herself the strength to continue. This is not going to end well.

"You were going to adopt him. We . . . we were going to adopt him. And then one evening you took him out, for pizza or something. And there was a drive-by shooting, and he got killed. You were sure that the bullet was meant for you, and that Bennett was behind it, because you had been after him. Getting him became an obsession from that point on; there is no way you would have gone off in a different direction."

It's a painful story to hear, but not because of any emotional attachment I have to it. Hearing about the death of a boy I can't remember is like hearing about any similar thing in the news. You feel bad, but you don't feel part of it. I don't feel a part of anything.

"Thank you for telling me that. But I don't remember the boy at all; I wish I did."

"I know. I'm not sure hearing it was the best thing for you, but I felt like you deserved it."

"You said that we were going to adopt him; does that mean we were engaged?"

She smiles one of the saddest smiles I can ever remember seeing. "Our wedding date was this Sunday."

THE *NEW YORK TIMES* RAN THE STORY ON THE FRONT *page.*

People that the public consider to be true heroes, those that have risked their lives to save others, are always latched on to by the media. This is especially true when the heroism takes place on American soil. There was probably no pilot in recent American history more famous than "Sully" Sullenberger.

Any morsel about heroes gets picked up in the press, regardless of how insignificant it is, or whether it glorifies them or brings them down. But when something major, truly newsworthy, is revealed, it creates a media firestorm.

The *New York Times* story on Doug Brock was truly a stunner, and it revived a story that didn't even yet need reviving. The headline was "Theater Hero Is Amnesia Victim," and the subheading said, "Has No Memory of Ten Years Prior to Shooting."

The headlines were slightly misleading, as any reader's natural assumption would have been that the amnesia came as a result of the shooting at the theater. But the story itself corrected that impression, and for the most part was reasonably accurate, which is the way Doug had instructed Jessie to tell it.

It reminded readers, most of whom needed no reminding, about Doug's being shot at the motel earlier in the month. It went on to say that what had been concealed was that Doug had suffered a brain injury that resulted in a case of retrograde amnesia. It essentially wiped out a decade of his memory, including the shooting itself and the events leading up to it.

Where the story differed from the truth was in stating that Doug's memory was slowly returning. It said that the recollections were coming back essentially chronologically, starting with the earliest, so he still was unable to recall the shooting or the immediate events leading up to it.

Without directly quoting any of them, it reported that both Doug and the doctors were said to be confident, based on his progress so far, that his full memory would be restored in reasonably short order. In their collective view, it was only a matter of time.

The article went on to state that at no point were his abilities to create new memories impacted, and he had no physical impairments, which was why he was on duty the night of the theater shooting.

The information in the piece was credited to anonymous sources within the department, all of whom did not wish to be linked to it by name. Near the end, the writer said that he reached Jessie Allen, Brock's ex-fiancée, who declined to contribute to the story. Attempts were of course made to reach Doug Brock for his comments, but he did not return the writer's repeated phone calls. His boss, Captain Bradley, joined the long list of "no-commenters."

Nowhere was there made any mention of the danger inherent in the revelations, that the people responsible for shooting Doug might be disinclined to sit back and wait for him to remember their role in it.

Nate was awake in bed the morning that the piece ran, and he was watching the *Today Show* as they reported on it. While a photograph of Doug was on the screen, Nate heard a noise and turned to see the actual Doug approaching his bed.

"Well, look who's here. It's the media superstar. Had I known you were coming I would have dressed up."

"It wouldn't help; you'd still look like shit. How you doin', big guy?"

"I'm living it up here in the fast lane; sucking down Jell-O like there's no tomorrow. I can't wait to weigh myself."

"So get your ass out of bed. I'm going to need some help."

"I wish I could," Nate said. "Doctors say at least a couple of weeks. They also said you saved my life; that you stopped me from bleeding to death."

"I was conflicted about doing it."

"Yeah, I bet. And I hear you nailed Sadri with one shot. Funny thing is that I can outshoot you any day of the week."

"Since when?" Doug asked.

"For years now. I'm the best in the department."

Doug doubted he was telling the truth, but couldn't know for sure. Either way, it certainly didn't matter. "You up to date on what's been going on?" he asked.

"I think so. Congers was here, and so was the captain. They filled me in. Gharsi and Sadri are both dead, truth and justice have won out again, and I'm lying here with a goddamn tube up my nose."

"Isn't it great when things go just right?"

"Yeah. I heard what you said about me at that press conference. Thanks for that, too. So they say you got your memory back? Does that mean I can't claim you owe me money?"

Doug walked to the door and closed it, so no one could hear them. Then he came back to Nate's bedside.

"It's total bullshit, right?" Nate asked, before Doug could even say anything.

"One hundred percent pure."

Nate laughed, and then winced at the pain. "I knew it as soon as I heard it. You want them to come after you."

"You got it."

He laughed again. "Memory or not, you're still fucking nuts. Did you plant the story yourself, or did you get someone else to do it?"

"Jessie did it."

By then he was laughing so hard that Doug was afraid he'd shake out the tubes that were attached to him. "I'll bet she jumped at it . . . a chance to get you shot. It's a win-win for her."

"She said we were engaged."

Nate nodded, finally getting the laughter under

control. "I was going to be your best man. It's just as well that it didn't work out; I couldn't find a damn tuxedo big enough. But you screwed it up big time."

"Hard to believe, since she is fantastic."

"Doug, I'm telling you this as your best friend, as someone who cares for you and only wants what's best for you. If you hurt her again, I will beat and torture you until you are begging to die."

"Thanks, that's what best friends are for."

"So what's your plan?" Nate asked.

"I don't really have one. I figure they'll come after me, and if I stop them, I'll trace the shooter back. If I don't stop them, then I won't have to worry about it anyway."

"Brilliant."

Doug nodded. "I thought so myself."

"Except with me in here, who's going to protect your vulnerable ass?"

"I'm self-sufficient."

"Yeah, you were really self-sufficient the day you did the swan dive from the motel railing. Just be really careful."

Doug was about to leave Nate's room when his cell phone rang. It was Captain Bradley with a question. "Is that story in *The Times* true?"

"Not a word of it," Doug said.

"Where did they get their information?"

"I don't know, but I wish I did. I'm pissed off about it."

"Get down here," Bradley said. "Now."

BRADLEY IS STANDING IN THE DOORWAY OF HIS OFFICE, *waiting for me, when I get there.*

The FBI guys seem to have stepped back, and neither they nor Congers are represented at the meeting. Gharsi was the guy that triggered their interest, and with him reduced to fish food in the Atlantic, they are only moderately interested in my situation.

And here I thought they loved me as a person.

Bradley calls in Jerry Bettis, who had been Dan Congers's partner when they were going after Bennett. Jerry is now the lead detective investigating the shooting at the hotel, which, because of the two people killed, is a murder investigation.

Bettis admits that the investigation itself is going pretty much nowhere. There were no prints of consequence in the motel room, no DNA that matched anyone of interest, and the bullets were from guns that were ice cold. Clearly, as Bettis points out, arrests are not exactly imminent.

But we are here to discuss the *New York Times* story

and its implications. Bradley is pissed about it; he's always hated leaks coming from within the department, and the fact that it was misinformation makes it even worse.

"There are two questions I want answered," he says. "Who did the leaking? And the more important one is, why?"

"I have no idea," I lie.

"It said in the article that it came from within the department," Bettis says.

I point out that the entire department knows about my condition, so it could have been anyone. "It could have been for any number of reasons," I say. "Maybe that reporter had done a favor for someone. Or maybe somebody inside told their wife, who told the reporter."

"I have made it clear from day one that nobody is to talk to the press. Once it starts, it steamrolls. It cannot be tolerated."

"I understand that, Captain. We don't want leakers in the department, but the boat on this has already sailed. We need to move on."

Bradley shakes his head. "You're missing the point, Doug," he says, unaware that I not only get the point, but I deliberately created it. "If whoever was in that motel room thinks you're about to remember who they are, they will want to make sure you don't."

"I can take care of myself."

"Maybe, maybe not. But that could be why it was leaked. To put you in danger."

"Good point. So let's turn it into a positive."

"How do we do that?"

"We wait for them to come after me, and we stop them. Then we find out who sent them, and why."

"So we make you a target?" Bettis asks.

"Yes. Otherwise we're spinning our wheels. And keep in mind, this might be about more than catching the shooter. This could be about preventing another attack like the one at the theater."

Bradley is clearly reluctant to go along with this, but Bettis takes my side by pointing out, "He's a target already; we might as well try and take advantage of it."

We eventually win Bradley over. "Okay," he says, "but we do this my way."

"Which way is that?" I ask.

"You're guarded at all times, twenty-four/seven, wherever you go."

"Great idea, Captain. We're trying to get them to come after me, so we do it by preventing them from coming after me."

"Those are the terms," he says. "Nonnegotiable."

"Okay," I say, even though I have absolutely no intention of adhering to the terms. "But tell them to stay as much in the background as they can."

"They'll stay where they need to stay to be effective," Bradley says, and then turns to Bettis. "You arrange the surveillance. If he gets killed, it's your ass." Both Bettis and I get the humor in that, but Bradley doesn't. He's not in a humorous mood.

"One other thing that is crucial," I say. "The fact that the story in *The Times* was bullshit stays in this room. As far as anyone is concerned, in the department or out, my memory is starting to come back."

"So you agree the leak is within the department?" Bradley asks.

"I don't know, but one person says the wrong thing, even accidentally, and the plan goes up in smoke. And that includes the Feds; I trust them even less."

Bradley agrees, and Bettis requests that I tell him where I am going to be at all times, in advance, so it will help him in arranging for my protection.

"You got it." Lying is coming easier and easier to me; I wonder if I've learned it over time.

Before I leave, I go to see Jessie in her office. "How did it go?" she asks.

"Perfectly. The captain wants to tar and feather the person who leaked the story."

"I'll keep that in mind."

"Sorry to put you in that situation, but you're the only person I could fully trust."

"You've only known me for a couple of weeks," she says.

"That's long enough. And Nate says you're the best."

She smiles. "He and I have a mutual admiration society. And he's helped me through a lot."

"I put you through it, and he helped you through it. He and I are some team."

As I'm leaving, she says, "Here, take this."

I turn, and she's holding out a folder. "It's the addresses for the rest of the list on your phone GPS. In all the excitement, I forgot to give it to you."

"Thanks; I'll get started on it."

"Be really careful, Doug."

GHARSI WAS NOT MUCH OF A DELEGATOR.

It all went back to his lack of confidence in the reliability and competence of those around him. He had long ago learned that whenever he could do something himself, while minimizing risk, things worked out better.

The upcoming operation would require, by definition, a large number of people to pull off. One or more of those people would likely fail, for any one of a myriad of reasons. The planning took that into consideration, and compensated for it.

An individual failure would slightly reduce the effectiveness of the operation, but the overall effect would be so devastating that it would not be noticeable to anyone other than Gharsi. The only failure that could not be compensated for would be if Gharsi himself were to fail, and that was not about to happen.

But there were certain aspects that simply had to be perfectly planned, and one of these was the choice of the targets themselves. Bennett said that he and Luther

Castle had surveyed the prospects and made the best choices, but that didn't impress Gharsi. No target could be certified as final without Gharsi examining and approving it.

In this case it had meant him working his way around the city, and being seen by literally hundreds of thousands of people. His change in hair color, and the addition of a moustache, would make it difficult to recognize him, unless someone was specifically looking. He doubted that many people, including law enforcement, had him top of mind.

Armed with a map of the locations, as well as a car that Bennett had provided, Gharsi had driven around the city. But unlike most tourists getting around with the help of a map, he was not interested in the sites a typical out-of-towner would want to visit. He was only concerned with parking garages. Underground parking garages.

There were seventeen on the list, and Gharsi was going to reduce it to twelve. It was an arbitrary number, but one designed to keep somewhat limited the number of people and the amount of supplies needed, without reducing the overall impact. Even allowing for one or two of the opportunities being aborted for whatever reason, the operation would have momentous consequences.

Gharsi knew that Bennett had turned the job of actually picking the targets over to Luther Castle, and Castle had been smart enough to only use self-parking garages, or at least those where the car's driver could actually get down to see the structures. When the time came, it would matter exactly where the car was parked; otherwise the effectiveness could be minimized.

Gharsi knew a lot about explosives, and a lot about the structure of buildings. Therefore, he knew where the explosives should be placed within the structure so as to do maximum damage. This was not a third world country; these buildings were well built, and could withstand a lot. Gharsi's plan was to hit them with more than they could survive, and that involved using both power and strategy.

By the end of that day, Gharsi had his dozen targets. There were three in Lower Manhattan, two on the Upper East Side, two on the Upper West Side, and five in Midtown.

Gharsi had taken a moment to think about the upcoming operation. People would be running in all directions, panicked, not knowing where they could find safety. The chaos would make 9/11 seem like a day in the park.

Gharsi couldn't help but smile at the thought. He hadn't realized that he was posing for a picture, taken by Doug Brock.

"HIS NAME IS DANNY PETERSON. HE'S AN INFORMANT *and a weasel," Nate said. "Not necessarily in that order."*

Doug had stopped at the hospital to ask him about the next address on the GPS list, a bar in downtown Paterson. According to the records, Doug had been at the bar for only fifteen minutes, but it was at two fifteen in the afternoon. That seemed to Doug like a strange time for him to have made a bar stop, and not enough time to drink if he did.

Nate was telling him about Peterson, and how they had called upon him at that bar a few times in the past.

"So you're sure he would have been the guy I was going to see?" Doug asked. "He's always at this bar?

"All day, every day. It's like his office. He hangs out there, does favors for people, runs errands, takes in and gives out information . . . he's like the vice president of Weasel-land."

"And we pay him?" Doug asked.

"No, he talks to us out of the goodness of his heart,"

Nate said. "Of course we pay him, but just like fifty bucks, maybe a hundred. Then he goes to the bad guys, tells them we were there, and they pay him as well. Peterson is an equal-opportunity weasel."

"If he's talking to the bad guys, why do we keep using him?"

"Sometimes he has good information," Nate said. "And sometimes we want him to squeal on us; that's how we send messages. Boy, are you out of touch."

"So if I want to get information to Bennett, Peterson is a guy I can talk to?"

Nate thought about that for a minute, then said, "He obviously would never get to talk directly to Bennett, but he'd get the information to Luther Castle, either direct or more likely through one of Castle's people."

"Castle was the other guy in the picture, right?"

"Right. He's Bennett's top guy; everybody reports in to him, and he reports to Bennett. Think of Tessio, or Clemenza, except Castle makes them look like Snow White and Cinderella."

"How long would it take for Peterson to get information to this Luther Castle?"

"With your rep right now? You say something to Peterson, and Castle will hear about it in a nanosecond. He'll be salivating waiting for you to leave so he can make the call."

Doug frowned; he knew he was asking questions he should know the answers to, but the experience bank was empty. "And what will Castle do?"

"If he perceives it as a threat, he'll tell Bennett and they'll send at least two of their people after you."

"Perfect," Doug said.

"Maybe, maybe not. They won't be sending a couple of college interns, you know? These will be experienced people. Of course, you used to be experienced too."

"I understand."

"There was a day you could handle them; now Castle will probably have you stuffed and hung above his fireplace."

"Thanks for the vote of confidence," Doug said.

"Why don't you wait on this until I get out of here?"

"Not going to happen," Doug said, and then asked Nate if he could borrow his cell phone. "You don't need it in here," he said.

"Why do you want it?"

"Don't worry about it. You'll get it back."

"Yeah, right," he said, taking the phone off the tray and handing it to Doug. "I should make you give me a goddamn deposit."

"Good-bye, Nate. I'll keep you posted."

Doug went downstairs, waved to the two cops in the car who were guarding him, and got in his own car. He didn't think it necessary to tell them where their next stop was, nor would they care. They would go wherever he went, sit in the car, and have donuts. It was an easy assignment.

So Doug took them to Tiny's Bar and Grill, on Market Street in Paterson, so that he could visit with Danny Peterson, affectionately referred to by Nate as a weasel. Doug's traveling companions pulled right up in front of the place, understanding that in this neighborhood, instant intervention might be necessary.

Doug went inside, and it took him all of ten seconds to identify Peterson, sitting at the end of the bar. Peterson actually looked like a weasel, small with a scrunched-up face. If that wasn't enough for Doug to know who he was, Peterson's reaction of stunned surprise clinched it.

Once he recovered, he got off the stool, turned, and walked into an adjacent room, leaving the door open behind him. Doug said nothing, just followed him inside and closed the door behind him.

"Man, I never expected to see you again," Peterson said.

"Why not?"

"You're a big hero now; I figured you'd be off making movies and shit . . . walking the damn red carpet. But here you are."

"Here I am. Again."

"I told you last time I didn't know anything," Peterson said. "I still don't."

"And I still want Bennett."

"I thought you lost your memory, or something."

"Yeah, well, it's coming back. And when it's all the way back, Bennett is going down, just like Sadri did, and just like Gharsi did. And you're going with them, unless you help me."

"How the hell am I going to help you?"

"Tell me what Gharsi and Bennett were doing together. I'm going to remember it anyway; it'll go a lot better for you if you tell me."

"I don't know what you're talking about. I never even heard of this Gharsi guy."

"Not the answer I wanted to hear, Danny."

"That's all I got."

"What are you going to tell Bennett when I put out the word that you put me on to Gharsi?" Doug asked.

"I'm serious, who is Gharsi?"

"Bye, Danny."

"Hey, come on, man. Give me some time to find out what the hell you're talking about."

"One day, Danny; you've got one day. I'll be back here tomorrow."

"Not here, man. I can't be seen talking to you like this."

The weasel was making it easy for Doug. "Then tomorrow night. Ten o'clock. The pavilion at Eastside Park . . . you know where it is?"

"Yeah, I know it, but that doesn't give me much time," Peterson said.

"It's all the time you're getting."

"All right . . . all right. But just you, not your boys out there." He had obviously seen the squad car pull up in front of the restaurant, behind Doug. "If Bennett's guys find out I talked to you, I'm a dead man."

Doug was happy to go along with the condition. "It'll be just me," he said. "Danny, don't screw this up."

"I NEED YOU AGAIN," IS WHAT I SAY WHEN JESSIE *answers the phone.*

"I'm listening."

"I'm going to be at the pavilion at the baseball fields in Eastside Park at ten o'clock. There will be some people there who could best be described as members of the opposition."

"So they took the bait?" she asks.

"Not officially, but I'm pretty sure they will. Otherwise, I'll be spending a romantic evening in the park by myself."

"What do you want me to do?"

"Just wait by the phone. When you answer it, I might talk, or I might not. Doesn't matter; unless I tell you otherwise, just call in backup on an urgent basis."

"Why don't I join you there in the first place? Maybe even the odds a little."

"Thank you, but no."

"I'm a cop, Doug. You used to know that."

"There are plenty of cops I could call in. This isn't

about you, Jess. I need to handle this by myself; that's the only way it's going to work. If they think I'm not alone, it will scare them off."

"All right. Ten o'clock, by the phone. How long should I wait?"

"One way or the other, it will be over by ten thirty. Probably before that."

"Then call me and let me know you're okay."

"I will."

"Be really careful," she says.

"That's the second time you've said that, and Nate used those exact words."

"That's because being careful was never your specialty."

I head home, tailed by my protectors. When I reach my building, I am glad to see that the parking lot in front is crowded, which makes my parking in the rear lot seem normal. Once I do, I open the trunk and take a quick look to confirm I have what I need, and then walk around to the front of the apartment.

I make a stop to talk to the two cops in the patrol car, and the driver rolls down his window. "I'm home for the night, guys, so you can take off if you feel like it."

"Not your call," he says. "We'll be here."

I shrug. "Suit yourself."

I hadn't expected that to work anyway, but it was worth a shot. It won't affect me one way or the other.

I find it interesting and a little disconcerting the way Nate and Jessie both felt it was so important to tell me to be very careful. It makes me believe that I must have been seen as a hothead, somebody prone to unnecessary risks.

It doesn't feel like I'm that way now, but I don't know if I've changed, or if they were wrong in their assessment. It's probably the former, and it might be as a result of my getting shot and having the resulting memory loss. I'm sure Nate's taking a bullet has contributed to my more cautious approach as well.

The reason it's disconcerting is that I feel like I'm an observer of myself, looking at me from the outside. I'm trying to figure out who I am, rather than knowing who I am. It is not a good feeling.

But what I'm going to do tonight, while some would lump it in with the overzealous label that it appears I've earned, doesn't feel like that to me at all. I think of it as doing my job, and doing what I have to do to survive.

These people have nearly killed me once, and they should have every interest in finishing the job. I understand that I've put myself in this position, but creating a lure to defend myself, to have the confrontation on my terms, does not feel crazy at all.

I've got four hours to wait until I have to leave, which gives me some time to think of all the possibilities. I believe I have most things covered, and if it turns out that I'm wrong, I will most likely be able to abort the operation. I really don't want to have to do that; it will just be delaying the inevitable.

One worrisome thing is that I remember the pavilion and surrounding area at Eastside Park as it was ten years ago. It had been unchanged for all my life before that, and I doubt that it would be any different today, but it could be, and I wouldn't know it. I should have driven down there and checked it out; not to do so was careless, another sign that I'm off my game.

I keep staring out the window, just waiting for it to get dark. My protectors are still parked in front of the building, just where they should be. They're probably taking turns sleeping, and counting the minutes until the next shift arrives. They don't know it, but by that point they'll be protecting an empty apartment.

When it's dark enough for my purposes, I take the elevator downstairs, and then walk down the hall to the furnace room. I enter it, and then go outside through the back delivery entrance, the same exit we used to avoid the media when I went to Trenton for the press conference.

I walk to my car under cover of darkness, knowing that my guards have no idea that I've left the apartment. I get in the car and start it, then pull out without turning my lights on.

I'm on the way, and I'm a little surprised that I feel a strong rush of excitement. Not anxiety, or fear, or even concern.

Excitement.

Nate and Jessie are right about me.

THE SKY HAS COOPERATED.

A thin layer of clouds has reduced the moonlight but left me with enough light to function. Paterson's traditional lack of funds for structural improvement has also cooperated, and the pavilion and surrounding area seem just as I remembered them.

The pavilion building is set between a large baseball field on one side and two Little League–sized fields on the other. I played on all of those fields very long ago, though it doesn't seem as long as it might, with ten years removed. I'm not aware of any function the building ever had, other than to house a snack bar that was infrequently open, and which sold nothing even close to edible.

The main reason I chose it is that it's virtually impossible to approach it without being seen. It's on the lower level of the park, and the road down to it is a long and winding one, dubbed by kids as Dead Man's Curve. The other entrance is off Route 20, but again it would be hard if not impossible to arrive unannounced.

I pull up close to the pavilion on the grass. It's illegal to park there, but no one is around to stop me, and hey, I'm a cop. I then go inside the building, using my flashlight to refamiliarize myself with the layout inside. It's just as I remembered it . . . basically one large room with no way in or out except through the front.

I leave my cell phone on the floor, about fifteen feet from the door, and go back outside. Then I find the darkest spot behind the largest tree and wait. It's well before ten, but if I were in their shoes, I'd get here early to prepare and get the upper hand.

If I'm nervous about any of this, I'm hiding it very well, even from myself. I'm closer to relishing than dreading the upcoming confrontation.

Exactly at twenty minutes to ten, I see the lights of a car coming down Dead Man's Curve. I'm going to be surprised and very annoyed if it's actually Danny Peterson, arriving as ordered. My expectation is that it's Bennett's men, tipped off by Peterson that I would be here, unprotected.

The car parks on the street about a hundred yards from the pavilion, and I can see two men get out. They are both large, much larger than Danny Peterson. They are murderers, but they are not weasels.

They approach cautiously, stopping to make sure I am not in the car. I can see a glint of light off each of their handguns. They walk past the car and right up to the pavilion beyond it.

"Come on out, Brock." One of them calls that out while they stand against the walls of the pavilion porch.

"Let's talk," he says, but tucked into the walls for cover, with guns drawn, they don't seem to be in talking position.

When they don't get a response from me, they look around to see if it's possible that I am not in the pavilion. But I am well shielded by the tree and the darkness, and they can't see me. Should they move this way and approach, I will shoot each of them in the head. But they don't. With my car in front of the building, they just take it on faith that I'm inside.

"Come on, Brock. Don't make this harder than it has to be."

I take out Nate's cell phone and dial my number. A few seconds later, I can hear it ringing from its vantage point on the floor of the pavilion. I stop it after two rings, as I would have if I were inside, trying to conceal my hiding place.

The two men look at each other, probably realizing that I could be asking someone on the other end of that phone to send help, and that they had better move quickly. They move quietly and carefully up the steps of the building, and go inside.

Once they are out of sight, I move to my car and turn the bright lights on, shining toward the building. Then I open the trunk and take out a canister.

I have no doubt that the two men can see the lights from wherever they are in the building, but just to make sure I have their attention, I fire a shot off the building's front façade. I sneak off to the side, facing the front, and away from my car, where they now must be positive

I am. I take the canister with me. In any event, the bright lights from my car will make it hard for them to look out and see anything.

I call out. "The roles are now reversed, assholes. Your turn to come out. And if you have your guns in your hands, you won't make it two steps."

Their response is to fire four rounds at the car. These are not the brightest bad guys in the world, because they neglect to shoot out the headlights.

When things quiet down, I call out to them again. "You don't really listen well. So try this: in a little while you're going to come out, but this time you'll be coughing and your eyes will be on fire. When you do, throw your guns out first, or I am going to put a bullet in each of your heads. I don't want to warn you again."

With that, I take out the canister and fire a round of tear gas through the window. I then take aim at the front door, figuring it will take about twenty seconds for them to appear. I've got to give them credit; it takes closer to thirty.

Finally there they are, choking and gagging, and seeking fresh air. "Throw your guns in front of you!" I scream while firing a warning shot. They both do so, and then fall to the ground, still gasping. They are lit quite nicely by the car's headlights.

I move toward them, gun drawn. I have a second handgun in case I need it, but I doubt I will. These will not be moving targets should I have to fire.

"Stand up," I command, and they do so with some difficulty. They're still feeling the effects of the tear gas.

I give them a couple more minutes to recover and breathe normally, because I'm a really nice guy, and then say, "Now let's have a little talk. Who sent you here tonight?"

They don't say anything.

"Okay, let's try another one," I say. "What were Bennett and Gharsi doing together?"

Still not a word out of them.

"This is my fault for not explaining the ground rules. I am going to ask you some questions. If you don't answer them, I am going to put a bullet in a place on your bodies. I'll alternate; first a bullet in you, and then in you. I'll call you Mr. Right and Mr. Left, and we're talking about my right and left, not yours. All set? Now who sent you here?"

Not a word; they seem to be unconvinced, or maybe still unclear about the rules.

"Boys, understand something. I know that you came here to kill me tonight. If these roles were reversed and either of you was holding the gun, I'd be dead, and you'd be heading off to have a beer. So nothing I do to you will make me feel bad."

I continue. "So this is the last time I'm going to ask you; who sent you here?"

They don't answer, so I shoot Mr. Right in the leg. I place the bullet just above the knee, because I'm also a caring guy. He screams in agony and falls to the ground. Having been shot myself recently, I personally believe he is overreacting.

I turn to Mr. Left. "Your turn," I say, "but let me give you a tip . . . you might want to try to cover your balls.

It probably won't help, but you never know. Now who sent you here?"

Mr. Left, quite possibly the brighter of the two, says, "Luther Castle."

"See? That wasn't so hard."

"If he finds out I told you that, we're both dead." Mr. Right doesn't confirm or deny that; he's still moaning.

"If you keep talking and tell me what I need to know, I won't say a word. And you'll still be able to father children. It's a win-win, except for the children."

"You made your point; you win this round," Mr. Left says.

"I win every round." I would compare myself to a current boxing champion, but I don't know any. I've got a hunch mentioning Evander Holyfield would make me sound dated. "What did Bennett and Gharsi have going on?"

"We don't know," he says.

"Uh-oh." I point the gun. "Left ball in the corner pocket."

"I swear, they don't tell us anything," he says, near panic. "Just that something big was going on."

"How do you know that?"

"They were recruiting people; offering huge money."

"How much money?"

"Seven figures," he says. "For each guy."

"For doing what?"

"I don't know. Nobody knows; there is going to be a meeting to tell the guys who sign on; everybody would hear it at once. But the deal is that once you agree to do it, there's no backing out."

"Where and when is the meeting?"

"I don't know. They haven't said yet. But I think it's soon."

"So Gharsi's death didn't end it?" I ask.

"I don't know anything about Gharsi, but whatever it is, it ain't over, that's for sure."

I ask some more questions, but I get very little additional information. I don't think there is more to be gotten, but I can't be sure. I could shoot them some more, but ultimately opt against it.

"Get out of here," I say. "If anybody else comes after me, I'll get the word back to Bennett that you talked."

Mr. Left agrees, though he and I know he is powerless to stop Bennett from sending anyone else to kill me. I watch as he helps Mr. Right to their car, then when they drive off I pick up their guns. I go into the pavilion and get my cell phone, not the easiest thing to do with the residual tear gas still in there.

Once I'm in my car, I call Jessie. She answers with, "Doug?"

"I'm fine," I say. "No need to do anything."

I can hear her audibly sigh in what I hope is relief, but might be disappointment. "Did you find out what you needed to?"

"Not yet, but I'm getting there."

I want to ask her if she would like me to pick her up so we could go out for a drink, but I don't have the nerve. I guess I'm willing to take risks about some things and not others. I drive home and park in the back, then sneak in through the same door I used to leave. The guys in front will never know I was gone.

All in all, it has been quite an evening. I suspect it says something about my character, and my condition, but I can't remember the last time I enjoyed myself this much.

"I CALLED YOU AT HOME LAST NIGHT," BRADLEY SAYS. *"You didn't answer."*

I called this meeting with Bradley and Bettis, and I'm already regretting that I did. "Sorry, I conked out early, and must not have heard the phone. I'm finding that I still need a lot of rest. Maybe I should start taking vitamins."

"Then I tried your cell," he says. "No answer there either. I guess if you could sleep through one, you could sleep through the other."

"Thanks for understanding."

"I'm an understanding guy, but I'm also a worrier."

"I appreciate that," I say, but I don't like where this is going. The fact that Bettis is smirking makes me even more sure I'm heading to the edge of a cliff.

"And because I'm such a worrier, I sent the two cops guarding you up to your apartment, to see what was going on."

I shrug. "I probably slept through the doorbell."

"I'm sure you did, so I had them get the super to let them in. You slept so soundly, you were invisible."

"I wasn't there," I finally and inevitably admit.

"Well, that's a fucking news flash. You mind telling me where you were, and why you disobeyed a direct order?"

"I was out doing my job."

"Your job is to do what I tell you," he says in a less than friendly tone. "And I told you to let those guys follow you, so that they can protect you."

"I'm sorry, Captain, but when I lead them around, I'm like the goddamn grand marshal of the Rose Bowl Parade. I can't get anything done that way."

"And what have you accomplished your way?"

"Quite a bit," I say, and I lay it all out for them. I leave out the part about shooting Mr. Right; it interrupts the flow of the story, and would also leave me drowning in paperwork.

"How did you get these guys to talk?"

"I reasoned with them. If I remember correctly, I was on the high school debate team."

Bradley calls Congers, who is at the task force offices, and briefly describes what is going on. Congers annoyingly but properly says that he needs us to tell the story to his bosses, so another meeting is to be convened in Bradley's office. It's to take place in two hours, a sign that they view this as very important.

Congers arrives with Special Agent Metcalf for the meeting, and I go through the story again. When I'm done, they start firing questions at me. "What makes you think they were telling the truth?" Metcalf asks.

I shrug. "I can't be sure that they were, but I would bet on it. I gave them plenty of incentive to talk."

"Did they claim to have seen Gharsi since the plane went down?"

"I have my doubts that they'd ever seen Gharsi, or even know who he is," I say. "Why? Is it possible that he's alive?"

"We don't have a body" is all he'll say in response.

"Do you have access to these two guys again?" Congers asks.

I shake my head. "No, this was a one-shot deal, literally. I don't even know their names. If they send other guys after me, maybe I'll get another bite of the apple."

Metcalf's turn again. "But they didn't give any indication what the 'big thing' that was going to happen might be?"

I am getting annoyed; they're talking to me as if I'm an idiot. "You think they might have, but I neglected to mention it?"

"You've been neglecting to mention a lot of things, like the fact that you were setting this whole thing up."

"While on the other hand, you've been briefing me regularly on everything you're doing," I say, and then, "What have you been doing?"

"Has your memory fully returned yet?" Metcalf asks, ignoring the question and the jab.

I shoot a quick glance in the direction of Bradley and Bettis; I give them a nod that it's okay to tell the truth. The stakes are getting too big to leave the Feds out of it; they have resources that we can't hope to duplicate. "The story that was in *The Times* was way off; I'm nowhere with my memory."

Congers asks, "Why didn't you tell us this before?"

"I wanted them to come after me, so I could break the logjam and learn something. Which they did, and which I did. And if you don't blow it, then they'll come after me again."

The meeting breaks up with a promise from me to start keeping everyone informed, though I don't mention that it's not a promise carved in stone. If I've always been this big a pain in the ass, I'm not surprised that Bradley suspended me.

I leave the barracks with my guard in tow, and head for the hospital to see Nate. Jessie is just leaving as I arrive. "How's our patient?" I ask.

"Not great," she says. "He's got some kind of infection; can't have visitors."

"Are they worried?"

She shakes her head. "They say they're not, and that they're just being careful."

I decide to take a shot. "You want to have a drink?"

"Doug . . ."

"It's not a date; it's a drink. Come on, we'll toast to Nate's health; you can't possibly refuse that."

She thinks for a few moments, and then says, "Okay. Where do you want to go?"

"Just tell me where we always used to go, and let's go someplace different."

IT WAS THE ELEVENTH SUCH MEETING THAT LUTHER *Castle had.*

To that point he had eight of ten people agree to his proposition. He needed a total of twelve, plus two alternates, just in case. Sort of like picking a jury, Castle thought, and the reference made him laugh out loud.

He was conducting four meetings each day; people showed up by appointment in the back room of the local bar that Castle used as his office. The meetings were spaced out, so that if law enforcement for any reason was watching him, it wouldn't attract undue attention.

This session was with Frankie Parelli, and for the first time Luther was approaching one of these conversations with mixed emotions. Parelli was young but possessed the qualities that made him a valuable employee; he was smart and tough, and not at all afraid to use violence when it was called for. He made good decisions, unaffected by conscience.

He was not someone that Castle was anxious to lose.

"I've got a proposition for you" is how Castle began all these conversations.

"I'm listening" is what Parelli would have said if he were talking to anyone other than Luther Castle. Castle hated wasted words, and he already knew damn well that Parelli was listening. So instead he just kept his mouth shut and waited for Castle to lay out the proposition.

"You should feel free to accept it or not; I don't really care much either way. We will have no trouble getting enough volunteers, so if you don't feel comfortable with it, I've got no problem with that. Understood?"

Parelli nodded. "Understood."

"Good. Your job would be to drive a car into New York City, and leave it in a parking lot. You will be told exactly where to park it. Once you've done that, you go to the Port Authority and take a bus back. That's it."

"What is in the car?" Parelli asked, though he had a good idea.

"Not your concern."

"How many people are going to die?" Parelli's concern was not really the potential human carnage, though he didn't think of himself as a mass murderer or terrorist. He simply knew that the death toll would be directly proportional to the amount of heat afterwards.

"Very few if any, because of the time of day the event is set for. The idea here is to make a point, not kill a bunch of pain-in-the-ass innocent victims."

"What's in it for me?" Parelli asked.

This was Castle's favorite part of these meetings.

"Two million dollars. A million when you've done your job, and a million after the event."

Parelli knew the event had to be an explosion, but all he could focus on was the amount of money at stake. "Holy shit," he said.

"Exactly."

"What happens afterwards?" Parelli asked.

"Whatever you want. You feel like it, you can retire and spend all day counting your money."

Parelli was stunned by the money, but smart enough not to be blinded by it. It didn't matter how much money he had if he was in federal prison, or lying on a table with a needle in his arm. "The heat will be intense," he said.

"There will be no way to trace it back to you, but if they do, we have a contingency plan."

Parelli just waited to hear it.

"When you get your second payment, you will also get plane tickets and foolproof identification documents, enabling you to fly to a country that does not have an extradition treaty with the United States. You would be free to stay there and live like a king, or you can return here at any time with another set of perfect documents. That would be your choice, but it is not a choice you are going to be faced with. Every contingency has been planned for."

"How long do I have to make up my mind?"

Castle looked at his watch. "About five minutes. Like I said, whatever you decide is fine with me. If you choose to be in, you're in for good . . . no backing out. But either way, you talk to no one about this other than me. No one. Violating that rule would not be a healthy thing for you to do."

"I understand," Parelli said.

"I figured you would. So make the call."

He didn't need five minutes. "I'm in."

JESSIE HAS A CAR AT THE HOSPITAL, SO SHE SAYS I SHOULD *follow her.*

She leads me to a bar in Edgewater called River's Edge, which I have never been to or which I've been to frequently during the last ten years. Your guess is as good as mine.

People pay fortunes to live in high-rise apartments on the West Side of Manhattan, adjacent to the Hudson River. They do it for the view, and while that is nice, the great views are on the Jersey side. That's because when you're in Jersey, you're looking at Manhattan. When you're in Manhattan, your view is New Jersey.

It's not that complicated.

The place is dark and relatively quiet, and not at all crowded. We get a table right by the window. Jessie orders a glass of Chardonnay, and I take a moment to think about it. It's been ten years since I've had a real drink, so I want to get this one right.

"Bloody Mary," Jessie says. "No salt. It's your favorite."

I turn to the waiter. "I'll have a Bloody Mary, no salt. It's my favorite."

"Spicy?" he asks.

I look at Jessie, and she shakes her head.

"Nope," I tell the waiter. "Not spicy is my favorite. I'm very particular. "

When he leaves, I say, "It's sort of nice not having to make decisions."

"No memory return?"

I shake my head. "Not yet. I wish I had kept a diary."

She smiles. "Not even close to your style."

"I shot someone yesterday," I say, in what has to be among the greatest subject changer lines of all time.

Her eyes register her surprise, but she doesn't ask me about it, so I continue. "In the leg; the person who owned the leg was there to kill me."

"Did it bother you?"

"Not even a little bit. But like everything else, I just wish I knew if that represented a new me, or the old me. What do you think?"

"I would say that if he was planning to kill you, then your reaction is the same as it would have been. I think most people would have that reaction."

"I may be the least self-aware person in America," I say.

"Which is ironic, because you never had any doubt about who you were."

I nod. "Okay, I'm tired of talking about me, and even more tired of thinking about me. Tell me about you; assume I know nothing, because that is the case."

"Doug, I can't do this. We're not on a first date; we're not on a date at all. I've seen this movie; I know how it ends. It's a tearjerker."

"I understand—we're just two friends and coworkers getting to know each other."

She seems wary, probably with good reason. "Okay, what do you want to know?"

"Where you're from, where you went to school, were you an only child, how was I in bed, that kind of thing."

"Brunswick, Maine; Bates College; one brother; mediocre."

I smile. "Feel free to expand on your answers at any point."

She returns the smile. "Thank you."

"What did you study at Bates?"

"Art history and modern dance."

"That's incredible," I say. "Those are my two favorites also."

She laughs. "I know even better than you how ridiculous that is."

"So you took art history and modern dance, and you became a cop?"

"My father was a cop, and that's what I always wanted. He wanted otherwise, so I went through the very expensive motions at Bates. It's a great place, but it didn't change my mind."

"What did your mother want?"

"I don't know; she died when I was six."

"I'm sorry," I say.

"That's okay. I haven't been six for a while."

The waiter brings the drinks, and she's right, I really like the Bloody Mary, no salt, not spicy. I also like sitting and talking with Jessie very much, but the only like I mention out loud is the drink.

We talk a lot about the department, and about her feeling dissatisfied with being typed as the "cybercop" when she really wants to be out on the street.

She is smart and funny, and seems better looking every time I see her. The old me obviously broke up with her, and hurt her in the process. The old me was just as obviously an idiot.

"Tell me about the case, or at least what you can," she says.

I lay it all out for her, everything that's happened. I don't have to tell her that the *New York Times* story was bogus, because she planted it.

She takes it all in and says, "I want to help."

"You've already been a big help."

"I want to do more. I want to do what Nate would do if he were with you."

"Bradley wouldn't go for it."

"Bradley wouldn't have to know. And I put in a while ago for vacation time next week."

"Are you going away?"

"No."

All of a sudden it hits me why she put in for next week as vacation time. I should just shut up at this point, but I think my injury has damaged the part of my brain that has any sense at all. "Next week was going to be your honeymoon. Our honeymoon."

She nods. "And now it isn't. Now I'm staying home and helping you."

"A different type of togetherness," I say, lamely.

"That's okay. I'm going to be a real cop for a week."

THE LEG WOUND WAS NOT NEARLY AS BAD AS IT COULD *have been.*

Not that Doug was aiming that way, but it had missed the bone entirely. Carl Swanson, the owner of the injured leg, formerly known as Mr. Right, was a large man. His partner, Jerry Daniels, aka Mr. Left, was even larger, but his belated willingness to talk to Doug had left him physically unscathed.

Swanson and Daniels had gone from Eastside Park directly to Dr. Thomas Rausch, a physician who had an ongoing relationship with all employees of Nicholas Bennett's "businesses." Hospitals asked questions of shooting victims, looking for details; Dr. Rausch considered them none of his business. He treated the wounds and injuries; he didn't question their origin. And he was very well paid for his efforts.

The wound and the treatment were painful, but that was going to be a day in the park compared to their upcoming meeting with Luther Castle. Castle had sent them to kill Doug Brock, and they had failed miserably. Castle would not be pleased.

So Swanson and Daniels nervously went to the bar in downtown Paterson that Castle often used as his home base. They went into the back room, where he was waiting for them, along with two other men that were on the same level in the hierarchy as Swanson and Daniels.

"Let me guess," Castle said when he saw Swanson limp in with Daniels. "Brock is still alive, and you have a bullet in your leg."

"Luther," Swanson began.

Castle interrupted. "Did you shoot yourself?"

"No. Brock shot me."

"Yet, if I'm not mistaken, you were supposed to shoot him."

Before either of the men could respond, the side door opened and Nicholas Bennett entered. They had actually only been in Bennett's presence once; the second time was unlikely to be a charm.

Bennett just took a seat and didn't say anything. He was going to be an observer. Castle continued, "You were about to tell me why he shot you, when I had instructed you to shoot him."

Daniels, not liking the way this was going at all, jumped in. "He got lucky; it won't happen again."

"Did you talk to him?"

Swanson and Daniels took a quick glance at each other, and Daniels spoke. "Not really; he ambushed us. As he was running away, I yelled that we were going to find him and fucking kill him. But that was basically it."

"You didn't tell him anything about what might be going on?"

"No. We don't know what is going on."

Castle looked at Bennett, who nodded slightly, got up, and left the room.

Both Swanson and Daniels viewed his departure as a negative. "Hey, come on, Luther," Daniels said. "You know we're stand-up guys. We keep our mouths shut." Swanson nodded vigorously in support of his partner's words.

"I gotta be honest, boys. I have my doubts. I think you told him everything you know. Mr. Bennett and I view that as disloyal."

It was nine hours later that a jogger in Pennington Park happened upon the bodies of Swanson and Daniels, wedged up against a Dumpster.

It was ninety minutes after that when the local TV stations broke the story, calling them mob-style execution killings. Doug Brock saw the report, and although he had not pulled the trigger, he was aware that he'd killed them both as surely as if he had.

He was fine with that.

IT'S A USED CAR LOT AND BODY SHOP, NOTHING MORE.

At least that's as far as I can tell, though the truth is that I can't tell much of anything, especially since I'm just sitting in my car in the parking lot.

The phone GPS said that I had visited this lot a few days before I was shot. I arrived at nine o'clock on a Monday night, and stayed for about a half hour.

I can't be sure whether my visit had anything to do with the Bennett case, but I certainly have no idea why I would have been looking for a used car. I called and asked Nate before I came here, and he said that I never mentioned anything about needing a car, and he couldn't imagine I would have bought one. I have the Crown Vic and my beloved Mustang. Also, a suspension from a job doesn't generally trigger a buying spree.

I am tired of blundering about in the dark, and sick of being frustrated. It makes me want to shoot someone, although I've already tried that, and it didn't really help.

Since I'm already here, I might as well try to accomplish something, whatever that might be. I get out of the car and go into the showroom. I want to see if any of the people that work there will react to my presence with surprise, or nervousness, or anything other than viewing me as a prospective used car buyer.

I walk around for a while, pretending to check out the cars. All three of the salespeople that I see approach and ask if they can help me. I don't see anything unusual at all about their reactions. The receptionist gives me a smile, but not a hint of recognition.

I wander into the service department/body shop and run into the same thing. I pretend to be interested in their prices for things that I say are wrong with my car, and I try to be seen by as many people there as possible.

If they've encountered me before in anything other than normal circumstances, they are excellent actors and actresses.

As I'm leaving, I stop at the receptionist. "Excuse me, how late are you open?"

"Depends on what night you're talking about," she says, giving me a big smile.

"Monday nights," I say.

"Six P.M."

"That's every Monday?"

"Every one," she says.

"What about the service department?"

"Five P.M. Every night except Saturday, when we close at one P.M. And of course we're closed Sundays. Would you like to make an appointment?"

"No, thanks," I say as I leave. If I accomplished anything, it's well hidden at this point.

I DECIDE TO CALL A MEETING OF OUR INVESTIGATIVE *team.*

It's not exactly a reincarnation of the Untouchables and would seem unlikely to strike fear in the hardened criminal community. It consists of an overweight cop lying in a hospital bed with tubes in his arms and up his nose, a jilted female cybercop who's on vacation, and a thirty-five-year-old cop who has no idea where he's been or what he's done since he was twenty-five.

We're meeting in Nate's hospital room; his infection has been sufficiently conquered to allow him to have visitors. I'm updating them on what's been happening, and hoping they can provide some inspiration for what I can do next.

When I finish, Nate is focusing on the two guys that just wound up dead. "Why would they kill those guys?" he wonders out loud. "I don't understand that."

"They screwed up," I say. "They were sent to kill me, and they failed."

"So what? They don't work for ISIS. And they aren't

old-time Japanese warriors who have been humiliated to the point where they want to go hang out with their ancestors. They tried, they lost, and they took a bullet in the process. Bennett should see that as 'no harm, no foul' and move on."

"Maybe he thinks Doug can link them to him," Jessie says.

"No chance; Bennett has layers of cushion between himself and anybody he uses. But even if these guys could be traced to him, so what? They could just as easily be traced dead as alive, and if they're dead, there's more reason for the cops to want to trace them."

"That makes sense," I say.

"Thanks for the vote of confidence," Nate says, demonstrating that his sarcasm ability has not been damaged by the bullet. "If Bennett was going to kill everyone who ever screwed something up, he'd run out of people real quickly."

"So what do you think it is?"

"Bennett must think they talked to you. Of course, if they admitted that they did, they are so dumb that they deserved to die."

"Maybe one of them ratted out the other, thinking he'd be off the hook, and Bennett saw it differently," Jessie said.

Both Nate and I consider that to be possible, and we don't have any better explanation. Nor does it really matter, since the two dead guys were out of the picture for us anyway.

"We have to assume they're going to come after me again," I say.

"Then get the hell out of here," Nate says. "I don't want to get caught in the cross fire. Been there, done that."

I ignore that. "The problem is that he'll just send more goons who don't really know anything, so we can't count on that as a way of getting information."

"What about the GPS records on your phone?"

"I'm running out of places to track down, and anyway, when I get there I have no idea what the significance of each place is."

"As I recall, there were a lot of New York City places on the list," Jessie says.

"That's what I'm going to check out next, though I don't see how it can be anything other than a waste of time. Based on the GPS report, all I did was wander around the city. I didn't spend more than fifteen minutes in any one place."

"Those guys told you that Bennett was recruiting people; maybe this was part of that," Nate says.

I don't think that's right, but once again I don't have a better explanation. "The thing that's bugging me is the used car dealership. You're both agreed that I wouldn't have been looking at a used car, particularly at a time when the dealership is closed. So the reason I was there has to be tied to this investigation."

"But that in and of itself doesn't make it significant," Jessie points out. "You could have been following someone, and maybe that person was buying a car."

"After hours?"

"Maybe he made a special appointment, or maybe he was dating someone who worked there, and she was working late. I'm not saying it isn't important; I'm just saying it doesn't have to be."

"We need to find a way to put pressure on Bennett."

"Why don't you throw him into another cabinet?" Nate asks. "That worked real well for you last time."

"That's one thing I wish I remembered," I say. "That must have felt good. Tell me about it."

"Not much to tell. He said something that irritated you, and you walked over and pushed him hard, and he fell back into a cabinet. I don't know how we got out of there alive."

"Out of where? Where were we?"

"In his office. I believe I've mentioned that you were nuts?"

Something about this is confusing to me. "Jess, I didn't see Bennett's office on my phone GPS. Did you not go back that far?"

"I went back to the beginning; that's a new phone, or at least you only started using it recently."

"Why?"

Nate has the answer. "Because when you got suspended, they took your department phone, along with your gun and badge. You replaced all of it with your own stuff, except for the badge."

"Can we trace my department phone before I got suspended?"

"I don't see why not," Jessie says.

"Nate, would I have been with you all the time?"

He shakes his head. "No chance. You were after Bennett twenty-four/seven; you even took a vacation week to do it. I'm telling you, all bets were off once—" He catches himself and stops.

"I told him about Johnny Arroyo," Jessie says, understanding his hesitation.

"Once that happened, you went batshit," Nate says. "We all thought you were crazy before, but you raised the nut-bar. Nobody could control you."

"How come you guys never tell me any stories about how charming I was?" I ask. "How much fun I was to be with?"

Neither Jessie nor Nate says a word, and I give them plenty of time.

"Oh."

JESSIE MUST HAVE WORKED ALL NIGHT, BECAUSE SHE *gives me the GPS rundown on my department cell phone first thing in the morning.*

I used it until my suspension, so that's where the report ends. It begins a couple of days after Johnny Arroyo's death, since that is apparently when I went off on my own crusade to nail Bennett.

As in the case with my phone, a first look at the list basically tells me nothing, as I don't recognize most of the addresses. My apartment, the barracks, and Jessie's house are on there frequently, which is no surprise. Also on there is a visit to the state prison, which I'm called upon to do occasionally, usually to question convicts.

I'm going to have to run everything down, and like before I'll be operating in the dark. It's frustrating, but as long as my memory is locked away in some room, there's nothing I can do about it.

I'm home this morning, trying to go through the

pages, eating cold pizza. My diet these days is pretty varied. I either eat hot pizza, cold pizza, or cold pizza that has been cold for more than thirty-six hours. The latter has lost some taste, and is very dry, but in its aging has gained some character.

The doorbell rings, or at least I think it's the doorbell, since I don't remember ever hearing it before. It makes a very light pinging sound, but since there's nothing else around that is a likely candidate for making that noise, I walk over to see if someone is there.

I take my gun off the table and hold it in the ready position, just in case. I look through the peephole and see a man, about my age. At first I don't recognize him, but then realize it's the guy from across the hall, the one that Nate and I ran into on my first day back here. I think he said his name was Bert Manning.

I open the door and he says, "Hey, Doug."

"Hello, Bert." He doesn't correct me, so I'm probably right about at least the first name. He seems a little nervous; maybe he's read about my memory situation and doesn't quite know what to say.

"Doug, can I come in for a minute? There's something I want to talk to you about."

"Sure," I say, and step aside to let him pass. As he does so, he sees the gun still in my hand; I had forgotten to conceal it. His eyes widen, and if he wasn't nervous before, I'm sure he is now. I put the gun in a drawer. "Sorry. Just being careful."

"No problem."

"You want some coffee? Or soda? Or water?" I ask,

but he declines all three. "What about some pizza? It's old, but it seems to be holding up pretty well."

"No thanks. I don't want to bother you, Doug, but . . ."

"No bother."

"I read about your memory thing. Is it all back?"

"I'm getting there. Something on your mind, Bert?" The answer to that question is clearly going to be yes.

"Do you remember the conversation we had a while back?"

"I'm not sure which one you mean. Why don't you tell me about it as if I don't remember, and if I do, no harm done."

"Okay. Well, as you know, I work down at the pier, in Newark."

"Right," I say, though of course I have no idea where he works.

"Anyway, I talked to you about something that was going on at work. At least I thought it was. You remember this?"

This guy is never going to get to the point. "Bert, don't worry about what I remember and what I don't, okay? Just tell me as if it's the first time."

"Okay, well, I didn't know whether to keep my mouth shut or not, I mean these are not people to mess around with, but when I found out about you and Nicholas Bennett, about how you were going after him, well, I figured you were a guy I could talk to about it."

"Right, and I still am." I don't know how he knew about me and Bennett. Maybe it was in the paper when I got suspended, or maybe I mentioned it, or maybe he has another friend in the department. Or maybe one of a dozen other ways; it doesn't matter now, and I'm not going to interrupt him to find out.

"Okay, good. Anyway, there's talk that Bennett is bringing stuff into the port, without it being examined, or in some cases even scanned."

"Explain to me how it's supposed to work," I say.

"Well, goods come in on these huge cargo ships. Before they're shipped, they're certified in the other country as to what they contain, and that everything is legal. These are big, reputable companies, sending goods in from friendly countries, so we supposedly can trust them."

He continues. "Anyway, it's like the honor system, and since we don't have nearly the personnel to check much of this stuff out, only random inspections are made. Very random; there's no other way. It's the largest container port in the world."

"You said something about scans?"

He nods. "Yeah, there's some tech stuff that scans some of the things that aren't inspected. I guess it can pick up drugs, or radioactive stuff, or whatever. I really don't know; they don't tell me about those things."

"Okay. Got it."

"Well, people say things, and the word is that Bennett is paying off a guy to make sure his stuff goes right through, completely unchecked, except for the scan for radioactive materials; everything goes through that. He might also be paying somebody off on the foreign end, but I can't speak to that."

"So it's just a rumor?" I ask.

"It was, until I saw it happen."

"What do you mean, you saw it happen?"

"We were unloading some cargo—it goes right onto these trucks in the containers. Anyway, this cargo was on a list to be scanned, and the order came down to switch things around. So this stuff went right through, and other stuff got scanned instead. There was no reason for it to have happened that way, at least that I can tell."

"Is that it?"

"No. The guy who is rumored to be doing this, he's a manager down there named Tony Gibbons. He's the guy who switched the scanning instructions around."

"When was this?"

"May seventeenth. The cargo that went unchecked was from Con-Over Shipping Services. It flies under the Moroccan flag, but ships from Spain."

"And you don't know where the cargo goes once it leaves the pier, right?" I ask.

He nods. "Right. The containers get loaded right onto the trucks, it's almost all automated. Then they go where they go. A lot of it goes by rail also, but the process is pretty much the same."

"Thanks, Bert; you did the right thing by talking to me about this."

"I just don't like the idea of drugs or weapons or whatever coming into this country."

"I'm with you on that." I find a paper and pen and start writing. "I'm going to give you my cell number. I want you to call me if you suspect anything happening again."

"You told me last time that you'd keep my name out of it," he says. "I don't need guys like Bennett knowing I said anything."

"You can count on it."

THE INFORMATION THAT BERT PROVIDED HAS *ratcheted the situation up another notch.*

It may have nothing to do with Bennett or my investigation, and it may be unfounded. For all I know Bert is jealous of this Tony Gibbons guy at work, and he wants his job.

If Bert's description is accurate, if illegal contraband of any kind is being brought into this country for criminal purposes, then this is way above my pay grade. This is a federal responsibility all the way.

If he had come to me before, as he said he did, then I would have certainly checked it out. I would have considered anything that could have implicated Bennett in something illegal well worth my time. And if I needed any further confirmation of that, based on the cell phone GPS records that Jessie just provided, I spent forty-five minutes at Port Newark two days before I was suspended. I don't know if I talked to Gibbons or not, but it's a pretty good bet that I was there as a result of Bert's giving me the information.

I discuss the situation with Captain Bradley and Jerry Bettis, and they completely agree that I need to go to Homeland Security with what I've learned. They're both skeptical that it's valuable information, especially Bettis, but they concur that it's a piece that we need to share. The Feds can determine if it means anything.

I call Dan Congers and tell him I need to see him right away. He agrees and says to come right down to his office, and that he'll have Agent Metcalf in the meeting. It may be a sign that Homeland Security has decided that I'm to be taken seriously when I say that this is not over.

When I get there, I'm brought into Congers's office right away. "Metcalf got called away on an emergency," he says. "Let's talk, but I can't promise that you won't have to repeat it for him later on. He might have additional questions; additional questions are a specialty of his."

"Okay," I say, and I get right to the point. "I have information that a manager at Port Newark is arranging to have certain cargo come in without being examined or scanned. And he's doing it on behalf of Nicholas Bennett."

"What is the source of this information?"

"An informant."

"Who might that be?" Congers asks.

"Sorry. A confidential informant."

"It's okay to share it with me," he says. "We're the good guys here."

"I don't share confidential information with anyone; that's how I did it ten years ago, and I'm not aware of a change in my policy. Anyway, it doesn't matter. The information is what it is."

"Do you have information as to what kind of cargo we're talking about, or when it came into the country?"

"I just know the date and the shipping company." I give him what I have, and he writes it down.

He nods. "Okay, it's worth checking. I'll put CBP on it."

"What is CBP?" I'm sure I should know that, but I don't.

"Customs Border Protection. That's what we call it now."

"What will they do with it?" I ask.

He frowns. "They'll do their job, Doug. They know what they're doing; if this Gibbons guy is dirty, they'll handle it. I'll make it a priority; I'll make sure they turn it around in twenty-four hours."

"Shouldn't this be a Homeland Security function?" I ask.

"They're part of Homeland Security. Everything is," he says with a smile. "We're taking over the world."

"How'd you get placed here?" I ask.

"Actually, I beat you out for the assignment." Another smile. "You were deemed not quite stable enough."

"I'm happy for you," I lie.

"Truth is you wouldn't have liked it. All I do is sit behind a damn desk."

"That sounds pretty good about now."

"Anything else, Doug?"

I consider whether to tell him about the used car lot, but then decide against it. Other than the fact that I know my phone was there, there is really nothing to tie it in, and certainly nothing for him to go on. So I tell him there's nothing else, and he promises again to deal with Tony Gibbons and the issue at the pier right away.

When I leave Congers, I wave to the ever-present cops assigned to follow me. Even though I've remained alert, I'm struck by the fact that Bennett has not made another run at me. Either he's learned that *The Times* story was bull, or for some reason he's no longer afraid of my memory coming back. Perhaps the operation is so far along that we can no longer stop it.

Of course, the other possibility is that he's just waiting for the right time to get me. It's something I think about every time I start my car.

I'm not sure what to do about Tony Gibbons and the situation at the pier. I've turned it over to Homeland Security, so I can't go down there with guns blazing. Congers promised to get an answer on this immediately, and I believe him, but I also know what bureaucracies can be like. If this goes to CBP and they treat it as just another item on a list, nothing will get done nearly quickly enough.

Based on the GPS, I was obviously down at the pier, but I have no idea why, or what I did there. If I caused any kind of commotion, or stepped on the toes of another agency, my guess is that I would have since heard about it. I don't know if I talked to Gibbons or not; the fact that Bert didn't mention it makes me think I didn't.

I head into Manhattan to retrace my steps of the day that the GPS says I spent there. It turns out to be even more frustrating than the rest of the stops on my GPS tour.

I travel all around the city. According to the GPS I spent very little time at any one stop. Jessie had warned me that it was an inexact science as far as the addresses go, and that problem is compounded in New York, where all the buildings are so close together.

I could have stopped in that large office building, or the coffee shop across the street, or the movie theater next door, or the fruit stand on the other side. Even if I knew the location I had visited, I'd have absolutely no idea why.

I had hoped that by being there, something would jump out at me, some inspiration would hit.

It doesn't. In fact, the only "things" that jump out at me are people who have seen me through the televised press conference celebrating my "heroism."

A young woman named Lillian Singer approaches and tells me that she's a booker for the *Today Show,* and they'd love to have me on any time to interview me about what she calls my "journey." She gives me her card, and I put it in my wallet while lying that I might be interested.

Being a hero actually makes it hard to get around; it would make me sympathize with today's actual celebrities, if I knew who most of them are.

The entire depressing day brings me back to Tony Gibbons and the used car lot. They are pathetic as leads, but they're all I've got.

The best thing about them is they give me an excuse to call Jessie.

"DINNER?" JESSIE REPEATS, WITH SOMETHING LESS *than eagerness and delight.*

Actually, she sounds like she's talking to her dentist's office, scheduling a root canal. When I called her I shouldn't have mentioned the dinner thing first. But I think I can recover.

"You said you wanted to help me on the case, and there are things I want to talk to you about."

"We're talking now," she says.

"These are not things we should discuss on the telephone; too much chance somebody is listening. Aren't you familiar with modern technology?"

She laughs, a definite good sign. Then, "This better be real, Doug. It better be about the investigation."

"I swear it is. I'll pick you up in forty-five minutes; make a reservation at my favorite restaurant."

"Which one might that be?"

"How am I supposed to know? By the way, where do you live?"

"I shouldn't tell you," she says.

"I'm a detective; I'd track you down. Besides, I have it on the GPS records."

She gives me the address, which turns out to be a town house in Englewood. I'm there in exactly twenty minutes, and she comes out when she sees me pull up. She looks absolutely amazing; the entire neighborhood seems to light up. I fight off the urge to turn and yell, "Eat your heart out!" to my protectors in the car behind me.

There are many things that have been hard to believe since I lost my memory, but at the absolute top of the list is the fact that I once pushed this woman away. I should have had my head examined well before I fell on it.

She gets in the car and directs me to a restaurant in Ridgewood. It's Italian, a neighborhood kind of place, and she tells me I love it. The owner gives us a big welcome by first name when we get there, so I'm pretty sure she's telling the truth.

The waiter comes over, and I say to Jessie, "Why don't you order for both of us, honey?"

She stares daggers at me, but does so. She orders pasta amatriciana for me; I'm not sure if I really like it or she's doing it to get back at me. I guess I'll find out.

After a little small talk, she says, "About the case."

"Yes, the case," I say, and tell her about Tony Gibbons at the pier. I say that the information came from an informant, but I don't mention Bert Manning. I completely trust Jessie, but confidential is confidential.

"I'm not sure if I did the right thing by turning it over to Congers and Homeland Security."

"You had to, Doug. This is not something you can deal with on your own."

"But now I'm in a tough spot. Anything I do constitutes interfering with their investigation."

"Let me take a wild guess," she says. "You're going to interfere anyway."

"Well, I was hoping you would."

"Excuse me?"

"I think we should focus on Tony Gibbons. If he's Bennett's key to bringing things into the country illegally, then it should show up somewhere. If he's on the take, then he's making a lot of money. That money has to go somewhere. We need a financial snapshot of Tony Gibbons."

"I'm not sure I like where this is going," she says. "Unless it's going to court to get a search warrant."

"We don't have nearly enough," I say. "A judge would laugh at us."

"No kidding."

"Jess, you're a genius with this computer stuff; you could get to this information, couldn't you?"

"I could, if I were inclined to break the law."

"I understand what you're saying, but this is important."

"Convince me."

"Okay, here's how I look at it. Two things could happen. One is we find out that he's not dirty, and we drop it. We don't use the information in any way; we forget about it, nobody is the wiser, and nobody gets hurt."

I continue. "The other possibility is we find out he's

dirty, and it gives us a roadmap to bringing him down, and maybe Bennett along with him."

"None of what we'd learn would be admissible."

I nod. "I understand that, and maybe at some point we'd get a warrant to get the same information, or maybe we just keep it to ourselves. Look, if Bennett and Gharsi were involved in bringing things into this country, there could be countless lives at stake. Gharsi is a terrorist; he's not bringing in marijuana."

"You're making huge assumptions here," she says.

"I know that, and maybe I'm wrong about all of it. I hope I am. But if I'm not, and we didn't do all we could do stop it . . ."

"Let me think about it," she says as the waiter brings our food.

I don't know how long it usually takes her to think about stuff, but I'm not about to push it. Instead I concentrate on Jessie and the pasta, both of which would be hard to improve upon. The only "business" that comes up during the rest of the meal is a mention by me of that used car lot in Garfield, and how I can't stop thinking that it has some significance.

It's a great evening, and I can say that I can't remember the last time I laughed so much, because I literally can't remember the last time I laughed so much. I drive her home, and when we pull up in front of her place, I can feel the awkwardness returning. So I decide to take over both sides of the conversation.

"Doug, would you like to come in?" I ask myself. "I really shouldn't; early day tomorrow," I answer. "Not even for some coffee?" I ask on her behalf. "Well, I do love coffee." It's not an inspiring conversation, but I'm carrying the whole load.

"You're pathetic," she says in an amused voice that makes the words not feel like an insult.

"I am very much aware of that."

"Did you ever see a movie called *Peggy Sue Got Married*?" she asks. "I think it came out in the eighties."

"No, I don't think so."

"It's about a woman whose marriage breaks up, and then something happens to her and she goes back in time, to high school. The guy she wound up marrying, who she still loves, is back there, and he wants to go steady, and someday to get married."

"You don't mind if I cringe during the rest of this story, do you?" I ask.

No smile from her; instead she continues with her movie review. "Anyway, all the old feelings for him return, but she won't let him get close, because she knows how it ends. So the question she has to answer is, knowing what you know now, would you do it all over again the same way?"

"Does she do it all over again?"

She nods. "It takes a couple of hours of movie time, but eventually she does. She follows her heart."

"And is there a happy ending?"

"I don't know; they never made a sequel."

Then something really terrific happens; she leans over and kisses me. And then, just to show that any moment, now matter how great, can be improved upon, she says, "You want to come in for some coffee?"

I WAKE UP AT SIX IN THE MORNING, AND JESSIE IS NOT IN *bed.*

That is my second choice; my first choice is to have her actually in the bed. Last night was amazing; I hope Jessie felt the same way. I'm sure we experienced it differently; for me it was the first time that we made love. For her it must have seemed like "been there, done that."

Actually, if I had lost eighteen years of memory instead of ten, the old Woody Allen line would have applied to me, and I would have been "reclassified a virgin."

I get up to look for Jessie; maybe I can coax her to come back to bed. I find her in the den, at her desk, typing away at her computer. "Good morning."

"Good morning," she says without looking up.

"You writing in your journal about your conquest last night?"

"Not exactly," she says.

"Then what are you doing at this hour?"

"Committing a felony."

"You're hacking into Tony Gibbons?" I ask.

She still doesn't look up. "Hacking is a very ugly word. But yes, that's what I'm doing."

"I must have been great last night," I say.

"The two events are unrelated."

"You find anything yet?"

"Just started. Give me some time."

I look outside the window, and realize that my "protectors" are out there. "Uh-oh," I say. "Those two colleagues of ours are going to know you slept with me."

"No problem. I've slept with pretty much everybody in the department. Now leave me alone; I have to concentrate."

There's a bagel store downstairs, so I get dressed and head down there. I bring back bagels and coffee; I'm feeling so good I even get some for my protectors. Jessie has her breakfast while she's working. She's very focused on this, and the last thing I want to do is change that.

"I guess I'll go down to the barracks," I say.

"Good idea. I should have this by early afternoon."

I walk over to her and rub her shoulders and kiss her on the head. "I had a nice time, Jess."

She doesn't say anything, just reaches and squeezes my left hand, which is still on her shoulder.

I continue. "Nate said if I ever hurt you again, he'll torture and kill me."

"He'll have to get in line."

On the way to the barracks, I pass a park where a team in uniform is practicing, apparently preparing for a game. The kids look to be in their early teens; I wonder if that is the team I used to coach, the team that had

Johnny Arroyo on it. Like everything else except Jessie, it seems completely unfamiliar to me.

Captain Bradley is not in when I get there, so I head for Jerry Bettis's office. When he sees me, he says, "Ah, there you are."

"You've been looking for me?"

"Yeah, I tried you at home, but you were apparently still on your honeymoon."

Clearly the word about Jessie and me has gotten around quickly, but I'm really not in the mood for banter about it. "What's going on?"

"We got the verbal report back from Homeland Security on your boy Gibbons down at the pier."

"Already?"

"Yeah. You need to get yourself a new set of informants. Gibbons is clean."

"Are you sure?"

"I'm sure that's what the report said, if that's what you're asking. The specific date you were tipped off on, Gibbons wasn't even there. His supervisor made the change in cargo inspection because the one that was checked was deemed suspicious. It turned out to be clear."

"Shit," I say, which sums up how I feel about it.

Since I basically have no idea what the hell to do now, I go down to the hospital to see Nate. I've been updating him on everything all along, and I find it helpful to bounce ideas off of him.

As soon as I enter his room, he says, "You gotta get me out of here."

"Why?"

"I'm fine, but they tell me I'm not. They say it'll be at least another week until I completely shake the infection. Just bring me a cake with a saw in it, and I'll handle the rest."

"Sorry, pal. Can't help you."

"Sure, you're out there shacking up, and I'm stuck in here watching soap operas."

"Who told you? Bettis? Why does my social life have to be the main topic of conversation among horny cops?"

"Jessie told me. She called about twenty minutes ago."

"Shit, I should have called her. I've got her checking out that guy Gibbons, and Bettis already got the report that he's clean."

"Bettis told you that?" Nate asks, apparently surprised.

"Yeah, why?"

"Because Jessie said she found something you'd be very interested in. I didn't get the idea that she meant he was clean."

I stand up. "Well, it's always a treat talking with you, but I gotta go."

As I head for the door, I hear Nate's voice behind me. "Take me with you. Please."

"THE GUY HAS TWO BANK ACCOUNTS," JESSIE SAYS AS *soon as I walk in the door.*

"One is a local bank in Elizabeth, and the other is one of those online banks. He doesn't use the online bank at all, except to put money in. He opened that account eighteen months ago."

"How much is in there?"

"Three hundred and forty-one thousand. And it's all been wired in there, from an account that can't be traced."

"Tell me more."

"He's got two cars—a Ford, which I'm betting he drives to work, and a Mercedes. He's also got a thirty-five-foot power boat. And if he paid for them himself, I can't find how he did it."

"Bettis told me that Homeland Security reported he was clean."

"Well, if he's getting all this cash from working at the docks, they must be swamped with applications."

"It doesn't make sense. Why would they whitewash him? This kind of stuff should set off alarm bells."

"They were probably just checking the activity at the pier. No need to look at his finances if he's not doing anything wrong."

"But the point is he was doing something wrong," I say.

She nods. "Right, but we only know that because your informant implicated him. Maybe Gibbons is able to cover his tracks at the pier. He must have access to the computer, so he changes these shipments, and then he is able to erase the fact that he's done so."

"So whatever is in the computer is reality."

"Welcome to the modern world," she says.

I nod. "And in order to have checked his finances, they would have needed a court order."

"Unlike us."

"Exactly," I say. "They're law-abiding, and you're not."

My cell phone rings, and caller ID shows a number I don't recognize. I answer it, and the voice on the other end says, "Doug?" The person sounds as if he is outdoors; I can hear the wind hitting the phone. It's hard to hear him.

"That's me."

"Doug, it's me, Bert Manning" is what I think he said, but he's either talking softly or we have a bad connection, in addition to the wind.

"Bert? Can you talk louder?"

"Hold on," he says, just as softly, and I wait for about

thirty seconds. "Is that better? I need to be careful; I can't have anyone hear me."

"What's going on, Bert?"

"You said to call you if anything was happening."

"Right."

"Well, it looks like something is happening. There's a shipment coming in today that's going to be loaded and moved out tonight at ten o'clock. Gibbons moved things around on the computer; it was supposed to be screened tomorrow, but that's not going to happen."

"Isn't it unusual for it to be happening at night?"

"It sure is; this is exactly the kind of thing I was telling you about."

I ask him for the information, and he gives it to me, but says I won't need it, since it's the only truck that will be leaving the pier around that time.

"Are you working tonight?" I ask.

"No. I'm at work now."

"Okay. Thanks, Bert, I'll take care of this."

"You're going to be there?"

"Someone will," I say, not needing to share my plans with him.

"Okay, but whoever is there, the truck will be coming out of the north gate."

"Got it."

"And you'll leave me out of it, right?"

"You can count on it. You did the right thing, Bert."

I hang up and relate the conversation to Jessie. When I finish I say, "We did this by the book the first time, and we got nowhere. Now it's on us."

"So you're going down there tonight?" she asks.

"I think Manning is telling the truth. If he's not, then all I'll have wasted is one night. But maybe we'll finally find out what the hell is going on."

"I'm going with you," she says.

"You don't need to do that. I'm not going to be going in shooting. I'll strictly be an observer."

"Which part of 'I'm going with you' didn't you understand?"

This is one tough lady. Not only can't I fathom why I broke off with her, I don't have any idea where I would have gotten the courage to do so. "Let me ask you a question," I say. "In past situations like this, when we disagreed on something, who would usually come out ahead?"

"I'm undefeated," she says.

"I'll pick you up at seven."

JESSIE AND I GO TO DINNER BEFORE HEADING TO THE PIER. We don't want to get there before dark, so as to make sure we're not seen. Since the truck isn't scheduled to depart until ten o'clock, we'll have plenty of time to get in place.

Before I leave I give my protectors the slip again. It's not exactly a difficult thing to do; I simply go to my apartment and go out the back entrance, the same way I did before. They are probably relying on my promise not to repeat that particular escape; they clearly know me even less well than I know myself.

Just as our "first date" wasn't necessarily a typical one, neither is this "second date." I brought with me a map of the pier area, just to be sure we'll know where to station ourselves. We discuss the plan, which isn't all that complicated. When the truck leaves, we're going to follow it, and then play it by ear, depending on where it goes.

We get there at nine fifteen, and fortunately the map has accurately portrayed the area. It's easy for us to park more than a block away from the north gate, in a very dark area. The sightline to the gate is perfect; if a truck comes out of there, we will know it.

By ten thirty, I'm feeling a little less optimistic about the plan. Maybe Bert was completely wrong, or maybe he was wrong on the timing, and the truck left before we got there. From where we are, it is impossible to tell if there's any activity on the pier at all; there's a decent chance that we are the only dopes in the area.

Then, just before eleven, the gate opens and a very large truck exits through the north gate. It's dark, but I don't think there is any identification on the truck, no company name emblazoned on the side. It turns right and heads east, and we pull out to follow it, staying a comfortable distance behind. There is no way we can lose a target this big and slow.

We follow it for a couple of miles, until it turns onto Route 21 North. I certainly have no idea where it's going; for all I know we could wind up following it to Canada. But I know where I hope it's going.

"Do you think we could be this lucky?" Jessie asks.

"It would be a pleasant change."

Sure enough, the investigation god is taking care of us, as the truck gets off at the Garfield exit. I'm so sure I know where it's going that I could pull ahead of it and let it follow us, but I avoid the temptation.

Within five minutes, it is pulling up to the used car dealership that I visited. "This is the place you mentioned, right?" Jessie asks.

"It sure is."

"The pieces may finally be falling into place."

"Now the question is, what do we do about it?"

As we watch, the truck pulls around to a loading area in the back. We have a partially obscured view of it, and I don't want to call attention to ourselves by repositioning the car. "Wait here," I say.

"Where are you going?"

"Just trying to get a better look."

I get out of the car and start to walk to my left, so that I can work my way around to where I can see. I hear light footsteps behind me, and I turn and see that Jessie has followed me. "I thought you were going to wait in the car," I whisper.

"That's what you thought, but it didn't work out that way."

We get a much better vantage point, but I can't say it gives us much better insight. At least three large containers are being off-loaded by the driver and at least two other men and taken into the building on forklifts. We have absolutely no way of knowing what is inside them.

Jessie tries to take pictures of what they are doing with her cell phone, but it's too dark to make anything out. I didn't even know cell phones took pictures; I wonder if cameras can make long-distance calls.

The entire operation only takes about twenty minutes, after which the driver gets back in the truck and pulls away. There's no sense in our following him; it's the cargo that has meaning to us.

We wait another twenty minutes, but don't see any sign of activity in the building. "Maybe they're sleeping there," I say.

"Want to go down and take a look?"

"I don't think so. There's no way to get down there without possibly being seen, and I don't want them to have any idea that we're on to them. And it's not like we have any legal basis to break into the place. This one I think we can do by the book."

We leave the area and I drop Jessie off at her house. When we get there, I ask, "Any chance that 'coming in to have coffee' line will work again this time?"

"Zero," she says.

"You sure? It was pretty charming."

"Positive."

I nod. "Then I'll hold it in reserve."

"Good idea."

When I get back to my apartment, I don't feel like sneaking in through the furnace room; it's really dark in there. So I just park in the front and walk over to the car in which my protectors are sitting, still under the impression that I'm inside. "Sorry, guys, I did it again," I say.

The driver nods and says, "Just don't get yourself shot. This is too easy a gig to give up."

The reason I am so willing to let them know I snuck out is because there is no way I am keeping the secret for more than a couple minutes more. I go inside and call the barracks, identify myself, and tell them I need to speak to Captain Bradley.

"Now?" the sergeant asks. "You think he works the night shift?"

"Please reach him at home."

"You know what time it is? This better be important."

"It's an emergency and can't wait. I'll take full responsibility."

He promises to contact him and within three minutes Bradley calls me. "Have a bad dream?" he asks.

"No, I finally had a good one," I say, and I take him through the events of the night.

When I'm finished, he doesn't even bother to reprimand me for breaking our deal by sneaking out. He immediately grasps the seriousness of this, as well as the opportunity it presents.

"Eight A.M. in my office."

"Good," I say. "We need to move quickly on this."

"No shit."

I HAVE TO ADMIT I AM IMPRESSED.

To this point it's seemed like everybody was tolerating me, and barely, at that. They've reacted to my efforts with something between indifference and amusement; at least that's how it's felt.

This time is very different.

Bradley clearly didn't get off the phone last night and fall back to sleep. When I arrive there at eight o'clock, he's waiting for me with Jerry Bettis, Dan Congers, and even Agent Metcalf from the FBI. To get them here, and at this hour, he would have had to convince them that this was important by telling them some of the facts.

As soon as we sit down, Bradley says, "I conveyed the basics last night, but you should tell them everything you told me."

I nod. "Okay. First of all, one of the managers down at the pier, Tony Gibbons, is dirty. I don't know who reported otherwise, but I'm telling you what I know to be true. He's driving around in a Mercedes, and he's got a thirty-five-foot boat, neither of which he paid for. I can't say for sure, but I'd bet if you check his bank accounts or under his mattress, you'll find he's got a lot of money tucked away. Unless I'm very mistaken, it's all courtesy of Nicholas Bennett."

I don't claim to have certain knowledge of Gibbons's bank balances, because I'm afraid Bradley will make the obvious jump to Jessie's involvement. It's why I didn't bring her to this meeting. This could still blow up in my face, and I don't want her to be collateral damage. If all goes well, there will be plenty of time to cut her in for the credit.

Dan Congers is taking notes as I talk; I would not like to be the Homeland Security employee who did the half-assed report on Gibbons. "He's covered his tracks down there pretty well," he mutters, to no one in particular. No one feels obligated to respond.

"An informant tipped me off that a Bennett shipment was coming in last night, and would be loaded on a truck and shipped out without being examined or scanned. This was arranged by Mr. Gibbons. I was there, and the information turned out to be accurate.

"I followed the truck to a used car dealership and body shop in Garfield. I believe that if you dig deep enough, you will find that it is owned by Bennett. I've learned that I had gone to that dealership after hours, before my injury, though I don't yet know why. It wasn't to buy a car; that much I'm certain of."

Nobody is asking questions; I've got their attention.

"I saw three containers off-loaded and taken into the building. It's possible there were four; it was dark there and I was watching from a distance. In addition to the driver, at least two people were already in the building, and they did the unloading. Then the truck pulled away, with only the driver. I stayed for another half hour, but the other two men did not leave."

I see Metcalf make eye contact with Congers. He must have conveyed some kind of message, because Congers nods, stands, and leaves the room. "Do you have any idea what was in those containers?" Metcalf asks.

"I do not. They certainly appeared to be heavy, but that doesn't tell us much. I do know that whatever they contained was brought into the country illegally, by avoiding customs. That in and of itself should be enough to get us a warrant to go in there."

As I'm saying that, Congers comes walking back into the room. He speaks to Metcalf, but loud enough for all of us to hear. "We'll have the warrant in twenty minutes."

"Just like that?" I ask. Apparently the process of finding and convincing a judge is easier in Homeland Security-land than it is in state police-land.

"Just like that," Metcalf says.

We spend the next fifteen minutes discussing the mechanics of what is to happen. It will be a joint Homeland Security/New Jersey State Police operation, with most of the manpower coming from our department. However, as Metcalf states very clearly, he is in charge, and will be making the decisions. Bradley seems fine with that.

Metcalf's first decision is one that I approve of: no one outside of this room is to know the target of the operation until we arrive on the scene. Bradley sends Jerry Bettis out to secure the necessary personnel; there will be a total of twelve of our officers, and Metcalf says that he will be employing six agents. Added to Bradley, Bettis, Congers, and me, that means a total of twenty-two law enforcement officers will be present.

I describe the layout in detail, and Metcalf issues instructions on how the officers will be positioned. He also sends an agent out to the scene, to keep an eye on the place from a distance. That will effectively remove any chance that the contraband will be moved out this morning, before we arrive.

Metcalf is an impressive guy; decisive and smart. As far as I can tell he covers every eventuality, leaving nothing to chance.

It's fair to say that for at least today, Garfield will be the home of the busiest used car dealership in New Jersey.

AT EXACTLY TEN AFTER ELEVEN, METCALF, CONGERS, *Bradley, and I enter the showroom.*

Metcalf walks to the receptionist, flashes his identification, and says, "FBI. Is the manager on the premises?"

The young woman seems very nervous; Metcalf's identification could show him to be president of the Mickey Mouse Club, and she wouldn't know the difference. She nods and says, "Yes. I'll call him." She picks up the phone, and a few moments later talks into it. "Pete, you need to come out here . . . now . . . please." Pete must question her as to why, because she adds, "The FBI wants to talk to the manager."

Pete comes out; he's probably in his early thirties, but looking worried enough that he's probably aged a year on the way here from his office. He'd be even more nervous if he knew that the place was completely surrounded by state police and FBI. Whatever and whoever is currently in this building is not leaving until we're done.

"I'm the manager," he says in a tone that indicates he'd be quite happy to relinquish the title.

"What's your name?" asks Metcalf.

"Peter Denorfia."

"Mr. Denorfia, this is a court-ordered warrant allowing us to search these premises. Please bring all your employees into this room, and instruct them to stay here until we authorize you to allow them to leave."

"Sure," he says. "Can you tell me what is happening?"

"I just told you what is happening," Metcalf says. "You are bringing your people in here, and we are searching the premises."

He nods. "I understand." He turns to the receptionist, who has heard all of this. "Becky, help me get everyone in here."

Including service people, salespeople, and whoever else, in a matter of moments they have fourteen employees in the showroom. Metcalf then nods to Congers, who goes outside and instructs all of our personnel to enter, and to begin searching the place.

I'm not part of the search team, which is fine, since I have no experience in it. Or maybe I do. Either way, I'm free to watch them in action, and once again I am impressed. They take the place apart; it would be impossible to do the job more thoroughly.

Every compartment is opened, every car is examined, both inside and out on the lot, and every possible secret room is searched for. It takes four hours to completely turn the place inside out.

And they find nothing.

Well, that's not entirely true. They find plenty of

cars—twelve in an inside garage and at least fifty outside—many auto parts, a large number of tools to use in repairing cars, and a whole bunch of tires. By the time it's over, it is a toss-up between who sends more disgusted and angry stares my way, Metcalf, Congers, or Bradley.

No one says a word to Pete or any of the other employees the entire time, other than granting them permission to use the bathroom. Finally, when the end of the operation is at hand, Metcalf calls Pete over.

"You received a shipment last night," Metcalf says. "Where is the material that made up that shipment?"

"You mean the tires?" Pete asks. "They're in that room over there."

"Are you telling me the shipment consisted of tires?"

Pete nods. "Yeah. We're about to have a sale."

Metcalf has Pete sign some kind of paper, and then we walk outside. Metcalf says something to Bradley, too low for me to hear, and Bradley just nods. I have a feeling he didn't say, "Great job, Captain. Your guy Brock is a good man."

Congers comes over to me and says, "Well, you set the tire smuggling industry back years today."

"Thanks."

"For what it's worth, I think you were right about this," Congers says, surprising the hell out of me. "I just think that somehow Bennett always stays one step ahead. I butted my head against the son of a bitch for years."

It was a nice thing for him to say, whether he means it or not, but it doesn't come close to making me feel better. I know I was right, but the evidence says I was wrong.

Congers heads for his car, and Bradley walks over to me, trailed by Bettis. At this point the only positive thing I can think of is that I took my own car here, and don't have to drive back with them. "You got any explanation for this?" he asks.

"At the moment, I don't," I say, because I don't.

"You are off this case," he says. "Write yourself a note, in case you lose your memory again. I'll dictate it for you. Doug. Brock. Is. Off. This. Case. Then underline it."

"I DON'T BELIEVE IT," JESSIE SAYS.

"I can understand that," I say. "But I was there, and it's absolutely the truth."

"So a crooked guy is getting paid big money to sneak tires into a used car dealership?" she asks. "And he does this under cover of darkness, to avoid the tires having to clear customs?"

"It's not possible, I'll grant you that. But I stood there and watched the whole thing. Those guys are pros; they searched every inch of that place."

"Then Bennett's people were tipped off. It's the only possible explanation."

I shake my head. "No. The decision to search the place stayed in the room with us. And an agent was sent out there to make sure that nothing happened before we launched the operation. They would have had no opportunity to do anything."

"Maybe they got rid of the stuff last night," she says, grasping at straws.

"Why would they receive a shipment, unload it off

the truck into the building, only to ship it out the same night? It doesn't make sense."

Jessie has run out of possible explanations, so she doesn't say anything.

"I'm glad you were there with me last night," I say. "Otherwise I'd think that not only have I lost my memory, but I've lost my mind."

"We know what we saw," Jessie says. "And more importantly, we know what we know."

"What do you mean?"

"There are a bunch of things that we know with certainty, and others that are close to certain. For example, we know you were shot because you were on to something important. And we know that Bennett sent those two guys to the park to kill you because he was afraid of what you might remember. And we're just about positive that Gibbons is dirty, and we know for sure that a shipment was sneaked through the pier last night without being examined by customs."

"All of that is true," I say.

"And I'm not finished. We've got a damn good idea that Bennett was involved with Gharsi, and that it had to be about more than blowing up the theater. Because what the hell would Bennett get out of blowing up a theater?"

"Money," I say, because I just realized that money is what this is all about.

"You think Bennett needs the money? I always see people like him as caring more about the power. The money may be a way to keep score, but the power is what they get off on."

"I agree with that. But money is a necessity for him to keep the power."

"And he's hurting for money?" she asks.

"I think he might be. I read the file, going back years to when Congers and Bettis were on the case. And it continued with Nate and me. We could never put him away; the lack of witnesses made that impossible. So we went after his money and we squeezed him. We made it much more difficult and expensive for him to operate."

"And it worked?"

"Seemed to, at least up to a point. Running an operation like his costs a lot of money. And he has a lot of competitors to fend off. The key to doing that is hanging on to the best people, and the key to doing that is to pay them well. There's no family loyalty anymore, if there ever was. Everyone is in it to make money."

"So where's the money in this for Bennett?"

"It has to be Gharsi, or at least the people behind him. It could be that those people pump their money right out of the ground."

She thinks for a few moments and then nods. "Okay, let's say I buy all of it. I still don't see how it helps us."

"I'm not sure it does, at least not in the very short term. But I think it will ultimately be helpful to know what Bennett's position is in all this. I think he's a hired gun; I think Gharsi purchased him and his organization."

"So we know, or think we know, why Bennett needs Gharsi," she says. "Why does Gharsi, or if he's dead the people behind him, need Bennett? What can Bennett provide them?"

"Contacts, the ability to operate . . . the pier is a perfect example of that. Bennett is the guy who owned Gibbons. And maybe Gharsi needs the kind of people that Bennett has working for him."

"Sadri was not one of Bennett's people," she points out.

"Which helps explain why he's dead. He was an ideologue, and an incompetent one at that. Bennett's people are pros."

"So where do we go now?"

"Back to the phone."

FOR GHARSI, THE RECENT EVENTS MADE A FACE-TO-FACE *meeting essential.*

He felt there was just too much going on, coordination was just too crucial, to leave it to any other kind of communication. Bennett and Luther Castle felt otherwise, but realized that Gharsi was not to be dissuaded. Gharsi had the money, so he was calling the shots. At least for the moment.

They met in a home in Woodcliff Lake, one that was recessed into the woods and had no nearby neighbors. The house was inhabited by the mistress of Luther Castle, and her name was on the ownership papers. But Castle owned the house, as he pretty much owned her.

Bennett and Castle were already there when Gharsi arrived, and they seemed considerably less stressed than he was over the latest developments. "What are you drinking?" Bennett asked when they settled into the den.

"We'll talk first and drink later," Gharsi said. "Where are my materials?"

"They are in a warehouse, under my control," Bennett said. "Well guarded, I assure you."

If Gharsi was assured, he was hiding it well. "Why did this happen?"

"We removed them so they would not be found by the FBI when they executed their search. We made fools of them."

"Why was there a search at all? Since you are so eager to give me your assurances, why were the materials not completely safe where they were, as you told me they would be?"

"One state police officer got in the way, so we adjusted. We always have a backup plan as effective as the original."

"This is the man you were unable to kill?" Gharsi asked. "Brock?"

"If it becomes necessary, he will die," Bennett said. "Killing him now would be counterproductive. He knows nothing."

"He knew enough to conduct the search."

Bennett smiled. "And now he is discredited. He is no longer a factor."

"This is not the first time I've heard that," Gharsi said.

"And it remains true," Bennett said, a cold edge creeping into his voice. "Now, shall we discuss our next steps?"

"Very well," Gharsi said.

"The materials will be moved back tomorrow. Then—"

"Back to the building that the police searched?"

Bennett nodded. "Yes. For that very reason it is the safest place to be. It will not be searched again."

"You are sure?"

Bennett glanced quickly at Castle, who nodded his agreement. "Yes," Bennett said. "And since the cars are already there, the chance of our attracting unwanted attention will be far less by keeping our plan intact than by improvising."

Gharsi took some considerable convincing that leaving the base of the operation at the car dealership was the right thing to do. There was no question it was easier, but he believed there would be far more chance of detection. He just did not have sufficient trust in what Bennett was telling him.

Finally, Bennett asked, "Are we agreed?"

Gharsi nodded. "With a condition."

"And that is?"

"The two of you are with me throughout the preparations." He smiled. "Call it a test of your confidence."

"You are not a trusting person," Bennett said. "It is an unpleasant aspect of your personality."

"Yet it has served me well. This is not negotiable."

Bennett glanced quickly at Castle and then nodded. "Agreed. Now let's discuss the delivery of the money."

"You are not a trusting person," Gharsi said, smiling for the first time. "It is an unpleasant aspect of your personality."

"Yet it has served me well. The money?"

"As agreed, half will be wired when I begin the assembly process. The other half when the soldiers depart with their cargo."

Bennett stood up. "Good. Now for that drink."

Gharsi had one drink and then left Bennett and Castle alone. "He is very confident," Bennett said. "He actually believes this will happen."

"He is stupid. Killing him will be a pleasure," Castle said, and then smiled. "And we will be doing the world a service."

THERE HAS BEEN ONE POSITIVE CONSEQUENCE OF THE *debacle at the used car dealership.*

Captain Bradley has removed my protective shadow; the police officers assigned to tail me are nowhere to be found. It was getting tiring having them around, and necessitated me taking evasive measures when I wanted to lose them. Not having them with me is sort of freeing.

What I don't feel is concern that I now might get killed. Part of that is likely due to my risk-taking personality, which everyone seems to agree is something I suffer from. But it's also a logical reaction to the fact that since that night in the park, no one has come after me.

It certainly wasn't because of my armed guard; any self-respecting killer could have circumvented them easily. Rather it seems as if Bennett must have decided I'm not worth killing, which both offends and puzzles me. If he was afraid that my memory might return before, why is he no longer fearful? Could it be that he thinks it's too late for me to stop them, no matter what I might know?

I head down to the hospital to seek Nate's counsel, to benefit from the insight his years of experience might provide.

"How the hell should I know?" he asks, when I pose the question.

"I knew I could count on you."

"You can count on me. Just lock yourself in a room until tomorrow, because that's when I'm out of here. Then you and I will deal with it."

"The doctors told you you're okay to be released?"

"No, I've still got a fever, and they say I can't leave until it's gone for at least forty-eight hours. I'm breaking out."

"Lying in bed and watching television doesn't appeal to you?"

"That part ain't bad, but I'm starving. The food is shit, and there's not enough of it."

I stand up. "This meeting has really been helpful for me."

"Where you going now?" he asks.

"New Jersey State Prison."

"They've got better food there; bring me back some. Why are you going?"

"Because according to my phone's GPS, I was there not long before I got shot. You got any idea what I was doing there?"

"No, but I doubt it'll amount to much. We were both at the prison a lot. Part of the job."

It takes about an hour and a quarter for me to get to the New Jersey State Prison in Trenton. I use the GPS to lead me down the turnpike to Route 9, and then into

Trenton. Even though I've been there many times, I don't remember any of them, so I'm just trying to avoid getting lost.

The prison houses a little over eighteen hundred inmates, and of course I don't know which one I was there to see. For all I know I could have been there to talk to one of the corrections officers. Nothing in my life is easy.

There's a reception/information desk with three people behind it. I walk to the young woman on the left, for the simple reason that the other two people are helping someone else.

As I approach, she looks up and says, "Doug! How are you?"

"I'm good," I say. "Really good."

"We're all so proud of you for what you did at that theater."

"Thanks."

"How is that memory thing . . . Hey, do you even know who I am?"

I might as well be honest, since once I ask her my question, she'll know the truth anyway. "Not yet; it'll come to me."

"Wow," she says. "That is really amazing. I don't know if I should be insulted."

"Don't be; it has nothing to do with you."

She leans in toward me and speaks softly. "I'm Mary . . . McCormick. We went out a few times. Then you stopped calling me."

"Hard to believe," I say. Mary joins the list of terrific-looking young women that for some bizarre reason I apparently decided weren't good enough for me.

"I got married last month," Mary says, possibly demonstrating that she rebounded quite well from the disappointment of losing me.

"Congratulations. My loss."

I finally explain to her why I am here. I give her the date and time that the GPS says I was at the prison, and ask her to look up who I was there to see.

"Was it an inmate?" she asks. "Because that's the only way I would have a record of it."

"I think so; I hope so."

Mary taps some keys on the computer, and waits until the information comes up. "Here you are," she says. "You visited with Oscar Filion, for about forty-five minutes. Oh . . ."

"What's the matter?" I ask.

"He's the man who was almost killed in an incident in the yard. He was stabbed."

"When was that?"

She types some more. "Three days after you were here. He was in the hospital for three weeks, and then put into solitary confinement for his own protection."

"I need to see him."

She nods, thinking. "Let's see what we can do."

IF LOOKS COULD KILL, I WOULD BE BREATHING MY LAST.

The look is on the face of Oscar Filion, and I notice it as soon as he sees me walk into the room. Since Oscar is a convicted murderer, I should be thankful for the limited ability of looks to cause physical harm.

Even though I obviously rejected Mary, she has been nice enough to set up this meeting on basically no notice. Because Oscar is in solitary confinement, we meet in a specially secured room. It's just Oscar and me, about to have a talk. No matter how much he hates me, hand-to-hand combat seems unlikely, as he is handcuffed to the metal table.

"What the hell are you doing here?" Oscar says in a tone that is pretty much a snarl.

"I need some information."

"That's what you said last time, and it almost got me killed. It also got me put into solitary. So thanks a lot, asshole."

I can't play around with this guy; he is too pissed off. "Look, I'm going to be honest with you. I got shot by one of Bennett's people, not long after I was here. It caused a head injury, and there are a lot of things I don't remember. So I don't know what it is we talked about."

"This is a joke, right?" he asks.

"I wish it was. I need your help."

"Last time I helped you, I got an ice pick in the gut."

"I'm sorry about that. I don't know if I had any part in that, but I can promise you I will do nothing to put you in any danger. And maybe I can nail the people who did this to you. I'm going to put Bennett away; next year at this time you'll be having lunch with him in the prison mess hall."

He thinks about this for maybe twenty seconds, then shrugs. "Nothing they can do to me now; I'm in solitary. And I'd really like to bury that son of a bitch."

Once again I have no idea what questions I'm supposed to ask, and less of an idea what I asked last time. "Great . . . we will. Let's do it this way: just describe our conversation the last time we met."

He frowns slightly; this is obviously nothing like any previous conversation he's ever had with a cop, or with anyone else, for that matter. "You started by asking me a lot of questions about Bennett, trying to figure out if I had information that could help you get him."

"What kind of questions?"

"Like were there layers between him and me. When I did something, like a hit, did I ever get the order directly from him."

"And did you?"

He shakes his head. "Nah. He went through Luther Castle, that prick."

"So you had all your dealings with Castle?"

"Yeah."

"And you think Bennett knew everything that was going on?"

"Definitely. Castle is with Bennett twenty-four/seven. If Bennett takes a shit, Castle wipes his ass."

That's a disturbing image, but I let it go. "So what happened between you and them?"

"They gave me a job, I don't want to say what it was, but I did it, and they shorted me on the pay."

"You don't have to tell me who, but was it a hit?"

He pauses momentarily, and looks around. I'm not his lawyer, so he's smart enough to know that microphones could be picking up everything he says. "What do you think?"

"Doesn't matter," I say. "What happened after they shorted you?"

"I complained, but they didn't give a shit. Castle told me I could take it or leave it. So I decided to leave it and go elsewhere."

"To the police?" I ask.

He frowns. "No way. What the hell do you think I am? I went to work for somebody else."

"You mean another crime family?"

Another frown at my ignorance. "We don't call it a 'family' anymore, but yeah."

"So they didn't like that."

He laughs a short laugh. "Yeah, that's one way to put it. They didn't like that. They tried to put out a hit on me, but that didn't work out so well. So they pulled something else."

"What is that?"

"They set me up to take a fall; they went to the cops."

"The police took information from Nicholas Bennett, is that what you're saying?"

"That's what I'm saying. Bennett is wired in ways you wouldn't believe."

It's a little hard to accept what I'm hearing. "So Bennett had knowledge of your crimes, set you up, and they didn't go after him?"

"You got it."

"Do you know who the cop was?"

"I know who arrested me, so yeah."

"What is his name?" I ask, cringing as I wait for the answer.

"It's Bettis," he says. "Jerry Bettis."

I'M STUNNED AND DON'T KNOW WHERE TO GO WITH THIS. I have no doubt Filion was telling the truth as he believed it to be, but that doesn't make it the actual truth. He could believe it and still be wrong. So before I decide what to do, I need to check the facts.

That is not as easy as it sounds. I don't know what I did last time with this information, but it might have been enough to almost get Filion killed. Of course, some prison snitch could have seen me and gotten word to Bennett that Filion and I met. Or his assailant could have had a grudge against him unrelated to Bennett. But I cannot assume that either of those things are true.

So at this point I don't want to talk to anyone about it, but I need some independent corroboration of what Filion said.

I call Nate in the hospital. "Nate, I need to get a look at a trial transcript going back four years."

"Which one?"

"Doesn't matter now; I'll tell you later." I trust Nate, I just don't want to take the time to answer the question now, since it would undoubtedly lead to many others. "Who do I know at the county courthouse?"

"Sue Pyles," he says. "She's the clerk down there; she'd have access."

"And I know her?"

"Know her? You went out with her."

"Any chance she dumped me?" I say, hoping that maybe this will break the pattern.

"No such luck. But I think you let her down easy. She doesn't hate you as much as the others do."

I head down to the courthouse, and to Sue Pyle's office. She greets me warmly; this shouldn't be a problem. We chat for a while, with me pretending to know what she's talking about. But she definitely doesn't hate me—in fact, she tells me that she brags to her friends about having gone out with a "hero."

I finally get around to telling her that I need to take a look at the trial transcript for Oscar Filion, but that I don't have the exact date. That doesn't seem to be much of a problem for her, and within five minutes she finds it.

It's an electronic version, and Sue sits me in an empty office with a computer terminal. "Let me know if you need anything else," she says when I sit down. She puts her hand on my left shoulder, and lets it linger there for a short while before leaving. Heroism obviously has its perks.

What would take me hours to find if this transcript were in hard copy takes me all of twenty seconds electronically. All I have to do is type "Bettis" into the search bar, and hit Return.

It's all there, just as Filion told me. Bettis testified at

the trial because he was the arresting officer. He was not on the stand that long, and his claim was that the incriminating evidence initially came in through an anonymous tip.

According to Filion, as related twice to me, the anonymous tipper was named either Nicholas Bennett or Luther Castle.

There is no doubt that the transcript enhances Filion's credibility, but it does not cement it. It's possible that he believed Bettis got the information from Castle or Bennett, when in fact it was really an anonymous tip.

Of course, there's another factor that increases the chances that Filion's story is correct. He most likely got an ice pick in the stomach for telling it to me. Ice picks carry their own credibility.

There are only two people that I can think of that I trust to share this information with. One is beautiful, smart, and great in bed. The other is six foot four, 280, and constantly complaining about lying in a hospital bed. The question of which one I want to talk with is the definition of a no-brainer.

I drive to Jessie's without calling first, so as to prevent her from telling me not to come over. My fear is that she might have come to view our lovemaking the other night as a momentary weakness, and she might have withdrawn back into her understandably protective shell.

I get to her house and ring the bell. I see the curtains part a bit as she looks to see who is there, and moments later she opens the door. "I really would love a cup of coffee," I say, because that worked last time.

She takes my hand and pulls me into the house, then kisses me. This coffee scam works really well.

I'm half expecting her to lead me directly into the bedroom, which makes me half wrong. Instead she actually makes me a cup of coffee; I may have been too convincing.

We sit in the kitchen and she asks me to update her on everything that has happened. I lay it all out: my visit to the prison to speak to Filion, and my confirmation that Jerry Bettis was the arresting officer.

"It's not true," she says. "There are some cops I would believe it of, but Jerry Bettis is not one of them. I know him very well; he's a straight-up guy and a good cop."

"Right after Filion implicated him, he was knifed in the yard. That's a pretty big coincidence."

"And that's what it is, a coincidence." Jessie does not easily abandon her friends.

"Well, here's my problem. I have to prove it one way or the other, and my first try at that got me shot. I should probably take a different approach this time, which is made more difficult by not knowing what the hell I did last time."

"Where was your phone after you talked to Filion the first time?" she asks. "Both later that day, and the next day."

"I'm not sure. I have the list at home in my apartment. I need to get it."

"You can go get it first thing tomorrow morning," she says. "I'll set the alarm."

Tomorrow morning is an excellent idea.

THE ALARM WAKES US AT 6 A.M.

When Jessie said she was going to set it for first thing in the morning, I should have asked her what she meant by that. I think she may be more of a morning person than I am, because she has already showered and is getting dressed.

"Get your ass out of bed," she says. I would have preferred "Good morning, honey, can I get you anything?"

I do as I'm told, shower quickly, and eat some pancakes she makes. They're good, but I prefer chocolate chip. "What are you doing today?" I ask.

"The first thing I'm doing is going with you to get the phone records. Then we'll decide after that."

"Yes, ma'am."

We go to my apartment to get the GPS records. I've long ago given up hope that they will magically provide the answer to my questions, and this time seems to continue the pattern. According to the locations that Jessie identified, I went from the prison to Centre Place in Newark.

"That's the FBI building," she says. "It's where Dan Congers's office is. He splits his time between there and our barracks."

I nod. "That makes sense; he was Bettis's partner. I could have gone to talk to him about what Filion said. Do we trust Congers?"

"We do," Jessie says. "Let's go."

I call Congers and tell him I want to come down and talk to him. He seems less than thrilled with the idea, but agrees. Jessie and I head for Newark, but she agrees I should talk to Congers alone.

I'm brought right back to his office, and he closes the door behind us. I don't know if he thinks we should have privacy, or he doesn't want to be seen with me. Or both.

"You really need to let us handle this," he says, even before I say why I am there.

"Handle what? You guys think this is over."

"It's never over," he says. "What can I do for you?"

"I came to see you here last month," I say, and I give him the date and time.

He seems surprised. "You got your memory back?"

"Let's just say I know I was here. I want to know why."

He seems to take some time to consider his words. "You wanted to talk to me about something."

"I was hoping for more specific information than that," I say.

He nods. "I know, but I'm not sure if I should give it to you. There's nothing to be gained."

"I'm going to find out eventually. I'd appreciate if you'd just make it easier. I'd like one goddamn thing to be easy."

He considers this again, and finally says, "Okay, you came to talk to me about Jerry Bettis."

"What about him?" I ask, although I basically know the answer.

"You thought he might be dealing with Bennett, that he might be on the take. You specifically referred to an arrest he made of one of Bennett's soldiers. I don't remember the guy's name; you may not have even told it to me."

"Do you know why I had these questions, or why I suspected Bettis?"

He shakes his head. "You didn't say, and I didn't really care."

This makes me feel a bit better. If I didn't tell Congers that I talked to Filion, then I wouldn't have told it to anyone. I was clearly maintaining confidentiality, which decreases the chance that I did anything to cause Filion to be stabbed in the prison.

"What did you tell me?" I ask.

"I told you it was bullshit. And the reason I told you it was bullshit is because it was and is total bullshit."

"How can you be so sure of that?"

I see a quick flash of anger in Congers's eyes. "Because I know Jerry Bettis. I know how he thinks, how he acts, what he does, and what he cares about. There is simply no chance that Jerry Bettis is dirty. I told you that last time, and I'm telling you that this time. Let's make this the last time I have to tell you, okay?"

"Somebody tipped Bennett off the other night, in time for him to get rid of whatever it was that was snuck through customs."

"Maybe, maybe not," he says. "But it wasn't Jerry; I'd trust him with my life. You may not remember what he is about, but I do."

This is his story and he's clearly going to stick with it. Just before I leave, I ask if I could see the report that said Tony Gibbons, the pier operator, checked out fine.

"Actually, I had meant to ask you the same thing," he said. "You indicated during that meeting that someone had reported him as clean."

I nod. "I thought Homeland Security checked him out."

He shakes his head. "Never happened. Who told you that?"

"Jerry Bettis."

I leave. Let him chew on that for a while.

I go downstairs, where Jessie is waiting for me in the car. "What did he say?" is her logical first question.

"That Jerry is a prince among men, that he would never do anything illegal, and that there's no chance he's on Bennett's payroll. He said he told me that last time as well."

"Is that it?"

"No. He also said that the report on Tony Gibbons, the one Jerry quoted to me, never existed."

"Those two statements seem to contain a contradiction," she points out.

"Yes, they do," I say. What I don't have to say is that the contradiction represents still another indictment of Jerry Bettis.

AFTER I LEFT THE FBI OFFICES THAT DAY, I WENT TO *the state police barracks.*

At least that's what the GPS list says, and it hasn't been wrong yet.

Of course, while the three most important things in real estate are location, location, and location, in investigations that is only a piece of the puzzle. It takes care of the wheres, but doesn't do anything for the whys, the whats, or the whos.

There is no way to know what I was doing at the barracks, and not even close to a guarantee that whatever I was doing had any significance to the matter at hand. The barracks is where I work, it's where my office is. I could have been doing paperwork, or bullshitting with the guys, or any one of a number of things that I would normally do.

I doubt that I would have confronted Jerry Bettis that day. Even if I had conclusive evidence, which it doesn't appear that I did, that would not have been the way to go. If I were to do anything in the barracks related to

Bettis, it would likely have been to tell Captain Bradley my suspicions and my evidence.

But that would have triggered some reaction, and word would have gotten out. At the very least, Bradley would have had to conduct some kind of investigation, and there would have been repercussions to that. None of it could have been done totally in secret.

Jessie and certainly Nate would have heard about it, and in fact I likely would have discussed the whole thing with Nate anyway. Yet he and Jessie have no knowledge of it. So it is very probable that I kept it to myself, waiting for additional confirmation, which I subsequently may or may not have gotten.

As far as Jessie knows, there have been no rumors about Bettis before or since, at least nothing that she has heard. Bettis has been promoted over the years, and is considered by everyone to be a fine cop.

I need to be careful how I go about this. For example, I'd sure like to know where Bettis was when I got shot, but I can't go about interrogating him about it. I have to try and go through records and logs, but I can't do that until Bradley lets me officially come back to work.

The problem is, I have the very strong feeling that there's no time to wait.

Jessie has been going over the GPS phone records, and she says, "The day after you talked to Congers about Jerry Bettis, you went to New York City. Seems like you spent most of the day there."

"I've retraced those steps; it was a complete waste of time."

"Let's do it again," she says. "Maybe I'll see something you missed."

"You won't. We're just spinning our wheels."

"Maybe you're right. But it's Manhattan; if things don't work out we can take in a show."

So we head for Manhattan, and after a couple of hours in the city, a show is starting to sound like a pretty good idea. Jessie sits in the front with the GPS records, and we start to cover the same ground I covered last time. Each address is just a place, be it an apartment building, a restaurant, a museum, whatever. There's no consistency, no rhyme or reason.

The fifth address on the list is in the Diamond Exchange, and we're almost there when Jessie notices something. "This is weird," she says. "The GPS records for the day you were in the city are erratic. They track you for a while, and then stop. They go on and off a bunch of times, but never off for more than a few minutes."

"So?"

"So I assumed that it was because of cell phone reception issues; you know, with all these high buildings maybe the signal gets blocked. But I've been checking my phone all day, and I've had a signal the whole time."

"Maybe some days are different than others," I say, no doubt demonstrating that I know very little about cell service. "Maybe the weather has something to do with it."

"Pull in there," she says, pointing toward a parking lot.

"Pull in there? It's sixteen dollars for the first half hour."

"Do it."

I pull into the lot, which is self-parking. She directs me to take the ramp downward, watching her cell phone as we go. When we get to the third floor below street level, she tells me to stop. "He was parking in each building," she says. "And you were following him."

"That doesn't exactly crack the case," I say as something attracts my attention.

"No, it doesn't. But it's a piece of information. Maybe at some point all these pieces will fit."

As we drive through, I notice it is much darker near the walls than in the center of the floor. When we get toward the end, I stop the car and open my door. As I'm getting out, I say, "Take my picture."

"What?"

"I'm going to stand over there. When I do, take my picture."

"Why?

"Please. Just do it," I say.

"Okay. Roll down your window."

"No. Through the window. Lean over to the driver's seat and take the picture through the window."

I get out and stand a few feet in front of the wall, where I might stand if I had parked my car there. Jessie snaps my picture, and I get back in the car. When I look at the photograph, it looks like a slightly blurry nighttime shot. I can see myself, but everything else is mostly black.

"What's going on?" she asks.

"We just got another piece of information. I think this might be where I took Gharsi's picture, the one I e-mailed to Nate. Now we have to figure out if the location means anything."

"How do we do that?"

"Well, for one thing, we're not going to get to see a show."

WE HAVE TO PUT THE ENTIRE DAY ON REWIND.

It means retracing all the Manhattan stops that the GPS led me to, but it has to be done, because now I have something specific to look for.

"What might that be?" Jessie asks.

"Well, we think we've learned a few things, which seem to fit together. One, that my photograph of Gharsi might well have been taken in a parking garage. Two, that if you get low enough in a garage, you lose cell service."

"I hope you've got more than that."

"I think I do, but I'll ask it as a question. If those two things are true, why would Gharsi go to a dozen buildings and park his car for five minutes in each one?"

I can almost see the light come on in her eyes. "Because it's the parking lot he was going to, not the building."

"Bingo." Then, "Do people still play bingo?"

"I think on cruise ships."

By the time we're halfway through the process of

checking out all the addresses, my hunch is proving to be exactly right. There are underground garages to each of the buildings, and just as importantly, they are all self-parking. Gharsi would not have had to just give his car to an attendant on the street level; he could have driven down there himself.

That proves to be true of all the locations. There are only three that are dark enough down there to have been the scene of the picture-taking, but I don't think it matters which lot I took it in. I think the fact is that the lot and buildings are interchangeable.

They are all targets.

We head for home, and on the way we discuss what we're going to do with what we've learned. "We're going to have a tough time selling this," I say.

She nods. "Especially after the search fiasco at the used car place."

"Right, but it's more than that. Playing devil's advocate, all we really know is that all the addresses I visited one day have parking lots. We can't be sure I was following Gharsi; I could have been sightseeing in the city. And we can't even be sure we have the exact addresses; you yourself said the GPS info isn't necessarily exact. And parking lots in Manhattan are not exactly a rarity."

"You kept losing cell service; it had to be because of the parking lots."

"Maybe, but again, that only speaks to whether I was there. It has nothing to do with Gharsi."

"We do have the picture of him," she says.

"Which we only think was taken in a parking lot,

because we believe all the other stuff, and that fits in. But there's nothing to identify the parking lot in the photograph; it's just dark."

"I know we're right," she says. "So where do we go with this?"

It's a question I've been thinking about since we developed our theory. It's definitely a matter for Homeland Security and the task force, and Congers did say he thought I was right about the used car lot. However, his boss, Metcalf, made it very clear how annoyed he was at the waste of time and resources that he felt I caused.

"I have more credibility with Bradley than with Homeland Security," I say. "Though not by much."

"And proper procedure would be to go through Bradley."

"I have a tough time giving a shit about proper procedure," I say.

"You never did. And then there is the issue with Jerry Bettis."

I nod. "I know. That complicates it."

We finally decide that I will talk to Bradley. That way I have two shots at the apple: if I'm not satisfied with his reaction and don't think he's taking it seriously, I still have the option of going to Congers with it.

Jessie wants to be in the meeting, but I talk her out of it. There just isn't any reason to involve her yet, and I don't want to jeopardize her career. I'm perfectly capable of conveying the information; having her there with me is not going to change the dynamic or the ultimate outcome.

I drop her off at home, and head down to the barracks to see Bradley. He's in a meeting, but I tell his assistant to get word to him that I have to see him on a critical matter. The message back is that he'll be able to see me in twenty minutes.

I wait outside his office, and Jerry Bettis sees me sitting there. He comes over, smiling and inquiring how I'm feeling. I tell him that I'm fine, that everything is good, and I leave out the part about my believing he is conspiring with criminals and terrorists.

When I finally get in to meet with Bradley, he opens the conversation with, "What kind of bullshit are you peddling today?"

As opening lines go, that is not a promising one, and it has the added negative effect of pissing me off. "Captain, I'm coming to you with something important because they tell me that I respect you. I don't remember respecting you, and at this point I'm having trouble figuring out why I would. So if you don't want to hear this, then just say the word, and I'm out of here."

"You report to me," he says.

"If that's what's causing the communication problem, then I'll quit. Is that what's necessary for you to hear this?"

He hesitates for a few moments, probably deciding if he wants to escalate the fight, or just hear whatever the hell I have to say. "What have you got?"

"First I've got a ground rule. When you hear this, you've got two choices. One, you can think it's bullshit, tell me so, and do nothing with it. Two, you can think it's important, and go to Congers and Homeland Security. Either way, you cannot tell anyone else, inside or outside your department."

"You think there's someone dirty in this building?"

"When I'm ready to go there, you'll know it. For now, you just need to agree or not."

"You're a pain in the ass," he says.

"I am keenly aware of that. Now make up your mind."

"Okay . . . this better be good. Tell me the damn thing already."

BOTTOM LINE . . . BRADLEY RESPECTED AND TRUSTED *Doug Brock.*

He was a good cop, as good as Bradley had in the department. Nothing Bradley had seen since Doug's injury had changed that, not even the incident at the used car lot. It was an embarrassment for Bradley personally and for the department, but he knew that Doug was acting on good, first-hand information. It just didn't work out.

If Doug was putting his job on the line, actually willing to quit to demonstrate his seriousness, then he must consider what he had learned to be important. And at the very least, it was worth hearing.

So Bradley heard him out. He heard about the retracing of steps in the city, about the self-parking lots in each building, and about the theory that Gharsi was in one of those parking lots when he was photographed.

He heard it all without interrupting, without asking a single question until it was over. Then he had a few, the first one being, "How do you know where you went that day?"

"Doesn't matter . . . I know," Doug said. Jessie had no legal authority to get his cell phone records without a court order, even though he had given her permission. There was no need to throw her under this particular bus, which was why he hadn't mentioned the dropped cell phone signals.

"Are you getting any of your memory back?"

"No."

"Do you know why you were following Gharsi?"

"No. It's possible he wasn't alone; he could have been with the person I was tailing," Doug said.

"But you don't know that?"

"I don't."

"Do you have a list of the parking lots you're talking about?"

"Of course," Doug said, and handed him a piece of paper with the addresses on it.

"Okay, so how are you reading this?" Bradley asked. "What do you think is going on?"

"I think these buildings are targets, and I think the bull's-eyes are the parking lots underneath them. The first attack on the World Trade Center was done that way, and it could have brought the building down if it were placed in a different position. I think Gharsi learned from that, and he's trying to bring more vulnerable buildings down all over the city."

"This is the same Gharsi that died in a plane crash?"

"This was before that. Maybe he has other people picking up the slack, or maybe he faked his death. We have to assume the worst."

"And the weapon they would use to take these buildings down? Car bombs?"

Doug nodded. "Yes. The kind of cars that you find in used car lots."

Bradley believed that Doug was wrong. He understood his concern, and thought it was absolutely correct for Doug to have come to him with it. But if he had to quantify the chances of this threat being real, he would put it at ten percent, probably less.

Of course, if he did nothing, and Doug was right, the consequences were easy to foresee. He had a quick image of the press conference he would hold after buildings came down all over New York:

"So you were warned this might happen, Captain?" the questioner would ask. Bradley would nod and say, "I was, but I figured there was a ninety percent chance it wasn't real, so I didn't do anything. I guess I was wrong. My condolences to the thousands of families on the loss of their loved ones. Next question."

Bradley figured that kind of quote probably wouldn't play too well, so there was no doubt that he would follow Doug's advice and "assume the worst."

"What's your choice, Captain?" Doug asked.

"I think you're probably misreading this, but there's also a small chance that you're right. So I'll take it to Homeland Security, on a priority basis."

"Thank you."

"Be careful," Bradley said. "If there's anything behind this, let the Feds handle it."

Doug nodded. "Works for me."

"You're lying and you're full of shit."

Another nod. "And from what I'm told, that's pretty typical of me."

Doug left, reclosing the door behind him and leaving Bradley to figure out the best way to do this. He would call Congers, that was for certain, and Congers would bring it to Metcalf. But just a phone call was not enough. Bradley had an excellent instinct for ass-covering, especially his own. He would call, but he'd also convey the situation in writing. If disaster struck, he would not lose a "he said-she said" confrontation.

There was a knock on Bradley's door, and it opened. It was Jerry Bettis. "I saw Doug come out of here," Bettis said. "What was that about?"

"Glad you came in; he had an interesting story to tell, and we've got to get a hold of Congers. I also need you to draft a letter for me."

"What's going on?" Bettis asked.

"I'll tell you, but I promised it would stay in this room. So the only person you talk to about it is Congers."

"I understand," Bettis said.

THE SECOND TIME THE EXPLOSIVES WERE DELIVERED *was very different from the first.*

They arrived the initial time in large containers on a huge truck, straight from the pier, late at night. So that there was no chance of attracting attention, this time they came in three enclosed pickup trucks, hours apart, during the day. Since the lot also sold pickup trucks, no one would have any reason to think anything unusual was going on.

Gharsi had by this time moved into a house in Rutherford, supplied to him by Bennett. Gharsi was not thrilled with the idea of Bennett knowing where he was staying, but he consented to stay there because it was convenient to the used car dealership. More importantly, Gharsi knew that Bennett would never turn on him, at least not until he got his money.

It would take Gharsi two days, arriving and leaving only at night under cover of darkness, to assemble and load the materials. He had relented on his earlier demand to have Bennett present for all of it, though he stood by his insistence that Luther Castle be there.

The explosives were called C-130, and they were of the plastic variety. Their power was awesome: on a pound for pound basis, their detonation force was more powerful than anything that did not result in a mushroom cloud. When well positioned in a building, as these would be, there were very few structures that would remain standing. And even those would sustain massive damage.

Once Gharsi arrived for the first session, the room with the twelve cars in it was locked, with him and Castle inside. The regular employees of the dealership were kept in the dark; they had absolutely no idea what was going on.

Castle was uncomfortable with being locked in with a devastating amount of explosives, but he respected Gharsi's obvious confidence and expertise. Still, he would be glad when this was over, and the loaded cars were out of there.

In two days, the men would be brought in, and they would be given their instructions. Then they would be on their way, and Castle would be a rich and powerful man.

And the world would never be the same.

I HAD A GOLDEN RETRIEVER MIX NAMED RIPLEY. SHE DIED *when I was twenty-seven.*

She was a great dog; I rescued her from a shelter when she was a puppy, and I had her for thirteen years. We'd go everywhere together; she made coming home to an empty house infinitely more bearable.

The day she died was one of the most upsetting of my life; she lay in my arms as the vet gave her an injection to end her suffering. But as devastating as that day was, it has taken on a new importance today, because of one simple fact.

I remember it.

I am on the way to Jessie's house, and I just saw a dog on the street that looked like Ripley. It triggered memories, including the day that she died. That was in 2007, the first thing I have remembered about the last ten years.

It is such an exciting moment that I almost crash into the car in front of me, slamming on my brakes to avoid rear-ending the woman, who stares daggers at me in the mirror.

I try to force myself to remember more, starting with other things about Ripley. I come up with some, but none after 2005. I feel desperate, trying to will memories into my head, but I get nowhere. I need to calm myself, to just let things happen, to let more memories flow naturally into my mind.

Nothing happens; I draw a blank.

When I get to Jessie's, she obviously can tell there is something important going on, but she naturally thinks it is about the case. "What happened? What did Bradley say?"

"He didn't believe me, but he realizes he can't take a chance on being wrong. So he's going to call Congers and let Homeland Security deal with it."

"And he won't tell Bettis?"

"I didn't mention Bettis; I told him not to tell anyone, and he agreed."

She stares at my face, her intuitive instincts raging. "What is it, Doug? There's something else going on."

"I remembered the day my dog died . . . in 2007."

"Doug, that's . . . are you sure of the date?"

"I'm positive."

"Is there anything else you can remember?" she asks.

"Not yet. I'm trying, believe me, I'm trying."

"Don't try too hard," she says, "let it come to you. You want something to drink? Maybe a beer? To relax you a little?"

She turns away and opens the refrigerator, standing there for a few moments without apparently getting anything out of it. Now it's my turn to trust my instincts. I go over to her and hug her gently from behind. "Unless

I remember that you're a serial killer, there is no chance I am going to be that stupid again."

She doesn't turn around. "You weren't stupid; you did what you felt you needed to do. When Johnnie died, you felt like you couldn't deal with it. You wanted to cut off from the world, from everything and everyone you knew and cared about."

"Things have changed."

She shakes her head; she's not buying it, at least not yet. "When you remember everything, when you have all the facts and feelings in front of you, you'll make another decision one way or the other. But when it comes to me, when it comes to us, I can't promise I'll give you that power again. You need to understand that."

I gently turn her around, and she lets me. "The only good thing about this whole experience is that it gave me a second chance with you," I say. "I am not going to blow it, believe me."

"As your doctor kept saying in the hospital, 'We won't know until we know.' "

That's as much as she'll give me on this, and that's okay. I'm going to have to prove myself as we go along, regardless of my progress in getting my memory back.

We finally get back to talking about the case again, and what we might do next. We've done our job in turning over what we've learned, complete with our theory. Now it's time to sit back and wait to let others handle it. That's their job.

"Sitting back and waiting has never been your style," she says.

"I'm starting to understand that. It's frustrating not

to be in the loop. For all we know, Congers and Metcalf could have told Bradley that I'm nuts, and disregarded what he had to say. That's if he's talked to them at all."

"We need to give them a little time," she says.

I nod. "Very little."

"So what now?" she asks, smiling. "Television? A walk? Maybe a nap?"

"I was thinking we could go to a motel."

THE PETER PAN MOTEL IS ON ROUTE 4 IN TEANECK.

It's about forty years old, and while it must have been a shiny new addition to the neighborhood back then, it's fair to say that its best days are behind it.

It's not convenient enough to stay in for someone wanting to escape high city prices; nicer and newer hotels have opened that are closer. Most of its customers now are people visiting family or friends in the North Jersey area, or salesmen here for a quick attempt to do some business.

I've passed the motel many, many times, but I've never gone inside, or even been on the grounds.

Except, I'm told, for the time I was shot and fell from a second-story railing onto my head.

I'm playing amateur psychiatrist here, in a desperate attempt to retrieve my memory. My thought is if seeing a dog that looked like Ripley helped me to remember the traumatic day of her death, then maybe coming to this scene will enable me to remember the devastating events that happened here.

Since Jessie was here that day, she's my guide down memory lane. "It's around the back," she says, so that's where we go.

We take the stairs up to the second floor and walk along the outside corridor, until we stop in front of one of the rooms. She looks around, trying to get her bearings. "I wasn't actually up here," she says. "Nate met me down below."

I look over the railing. The height is not that significant, but the chance of injury is somewhat increased when the person falling lands on his head, rather than his feet.

"Here we are," she says, walking a few more yards. "I'm pretty sure this is the room." She then goes to the railing. "This is where you fell; you landed down there. I think the bodies of the two people that were murdered were over there."

I try to take it all in. I look into the room, and the adjacent ones. I walk to the railing where I was shot. I assume I must have left some blood behind, but it has been cleaned up.

I look over the railing and down, trying to imagine the feeling of falling. I walk back down to where I landed, trying to re-create the feeling of lying there, even though I am certain I must have been unconscious then.

I'm increasingly desperate; I won't say that panic is setting in, but it's getting close. Every instinct in my body tells me that something terrible is about to happen, simply because I can't get my goddamn mind to work. I envision a day, maybe a week or month after the disaster, when it all finally comes to me. I don't know how I will be able to handle that.

"Try and relax, Doug," Jessie says, once again successfully reading my mind. I just wish she could read it well enough to tell me what the hell happened that day.

I repeat the process, looking in the rooms, over the rail, forcing myself to relive that day, screaming at my brain to start functioning.

But it won't.

I can't remember anything.

I NEED TO FIND OUT WHAT IS GOING ON.

Just sitting around and hoping that Congers and Homeland Security are taking me seriously is not getting it done. I need to know what is happening, in real time.

I drop Jessie off and head back down to the barracks to talk to Bradley. If he can't update me I'll go to Congers, then Metcalf, and eventually work my way up to the president if necessary.

When I get to Bradley's office, he says, "Please tell me you're just here for a visit."

"I'm just here for a visit. What did Congers say?"

"That they would look into it."

"That's it?" I ask.

"What did you expect him to say?"

"So did they look into it?"

"I don't know; I haven't heard anything back. Check with Bettis."

I find it hard to believe that he just said what I think he said. "Why would I check with Bettis?"

"I told him to follow up with Congers."

"Our agreement was that you would tell no one other than Congers and Metcalf."

Bradley looks genuinely surprised. "Bettis is running the investigation, Doug. Why would you want me not to tell him?"

"He's running what investigation?"

"The shooting at the motel."

I am furious, trying to control myself. "Yeah? How the hell is that working out?"

"What is your problem?" he asks, not backing down.

I don't want to tell him what I suspect about Bettis, because he's not going to believe me. The word will get back to Bettis, and any advantage we have will get wiped out.

"My problem is that your promises don't mean shit," I say.

Bradley says something in response, but I'm not sure what it is, because I'm already out the door, slamming it behind me.

Going to Bradley in the first place was a mistake; I know that now. I'm the one who thinks I have the answer, and I'm the only one who can convey it in a way that has any chance of it getting treated with the importance it deserves.

I should have gone to Congers myself, which is what I am going to do now.

Congers is out when I get to his office, so I ask to speak to Metcalf. I'm told that he is in meetings and can't be interrupted, so I'm about to set fire to the damn place when Congers finally shows up. He brings me into his office and asks, "This about Jerry Bettis again?"

"Much bigger."

"This the parking lot theory?"

Well, at least I now know that Bradley actually talked to him about it. "You need to take this seriously," I say.

"Doug, we take everything seriously. Homeland Security is all about taking everything seriously. There should be a sign above the damn door that says 'We take everything seriously.' "

"So what are you doing about it?"

"We're running it down."

I'm rapidly finding this conversation to be almost as frustrating as the one I just had with Bradley. "What does that mean?"

"You know how many tips we get into this department, Doug? Every day? Hundreds. Every week? Thousands. And we run down every one that has even an iota of credibility. Because the one we don't treat as important, that's the one that's going to bite us in the ass. We can't afford to be wrong, not even once. Unlike you—being wrong doesn't seem to bother you at all."

"So this is on a list somewhere?"

"It is."

"Do you prioritize?"

"Of course."

"Then this should be on top of the list."

"The last time, when we searched the used car place, that was on the top of the list. You were number one with a bullet. This time you didn't quite make it that high. In case you don't remember, we found nothing."

"We found plenty of weapons, but we didn't recognize them. The cars are the weapons; they just weren't armed yet."

"Come on, Doug, what have you got? You drove around New York, parking your car? That's it? You think you took the picture of Gharsi in a garage? Well, let me tell you something. Our experts think that picture could have been taken anywhere; there is nothing other than your hunch that says it was in a garage. And what if it was? Gharsi, who is currently at the bottom of the Atlantic Ocean, parked in a garage? That's the key to breaking the case? And you're the only one who even thinks there is a case."

I'm trying to keep my composure, but the stress of trying to remember, plus the greater stress of dealing with people who don't believe me, is starting to get to me. "You need to make this a priority," I say, trying to unclench my teeth as I talk.

"We'll run it down like we run down everything, Doug. In the meantime, I think you'd be well advised to take a rest. You've been through a lot."

"What the hell are you talking about?"

"You come in here accusing Jerry Bettis, one of the best cops I know. Then you get the idea that a used car shop is a goddamn arsenal, and that the world is coming to an end. You're losing it, Doug."

"Was I losing it at the movie theater?" I ask.

"No, you did great with that. But it's been downhill ever since. Maybe the hero worship is messing with your mind."

"That is bullshit."

He sighs, like he tried and failed. "Okay, do what you want. Now, is there anything else?"

"Yeah," I say, looking at my watch for effect. "You've got thirty-six hours, until first thing Thursday morning. And I really shouldn't give you that much time."

"To do what?"

"To check this out, fully and completely, and tell me what you learned."

Congers shakes his head, as if saddened by what he is hearing. "Get out of here, Doug. You're starting to bore me."

"Thirty-six hours," I repeat.

"Or you'll do what?"

"I'll go on the goddamn *Today Show, Good Morning America,* and CNN, and lay out the whole thing. I'm a hero, remember? People will listen to whatever I have to say. And what I'll say is that we're about to be under attack, and you and your buddies aren't doing shit about it."

With that I turn and leave.

That felt good.

I feel a little better now.

"DO YOU THINK YOU SCARED HIM INTO DOING *something?" Jessie asks.*

We're in Nate's hospital room, with Jessie on one side of his bed and me on the other. I shrug. "I don't know; I should have waited around to find out. But I made a hell of a dramatic exit."

She laughs. "I'll bet you did. But will you follow through on the threat?"

Before I can answer, Nate nods. "Unless his personality has done a one eighty, he will follow through on the threat."

"Damn right. Can you imagine what would happen if I went on national TV and said there was about to be an attack on a bunch of buildings in New York, and that it was going to be launched from a used car dealership in Garfield? Within an hour five million people would leave Manhattan, and another million would head to Garfield to check the place out. They'd be selling 'Garfield Versus the World' T-Shirts."

"Then what if we're wrong?" Jessie asks.

"The public's view of me would change pretty quickly. I'd go from being O. J. Simpson to being O. J. Simpson."

She smiles. "I was thinking Lance Armstrong to Lance Armstrong."

"Why? What happened to him?"

"At some point you'll remember. So what do we do now?"

"There aren't a lot of great options. If Bettis knows what we're doing, it might be worthwhile to follow him. And I guess I could keep an eye on the car dealership. Although Bettis finding out what we know could have caused them to move the location they're going to use."

"Jerry is not involved," Nate says. "No chance."

Jessie agrees. "That's what I told him."

"Maybe you'll both turn out to be right. But I'm operating under the assumption that he is. We get nowhere by thinking otherwise."

The hospital food services person comes in with Nate's meal. Nate lifts the lid off and looks under it. He makes a face and puts the lid back. "Here's something you can do while you're waiting for Congers. Get me a pastrami sandwich. On rye with mustard. With a pickle."

We both ignore that request, and Jessie says, "Here's what I think we should do. You follow Bettis, and I'll stake out the car dealership. In a perfect world, he'll lead you right to me."

I'd rather leave Jessie out of this kind of thing, but that's because I keep forgetting that she's a cop, and Nate says she's a damn good one. I don't remember her in that context, but I need to start accepting it.

"Okay. But you'll call me if there's any activity before you do anything about it, right?"

"Yes, O powerful male."

I turn to Nate. "We're a little shorthanded as far as the investigation goes. When are you finally going to get your fat ass out of here?"

"Why? You got something for me?"

"Nothing crucial, but I'd like to get a look at the murder book for the Filion case. All I have is Bettis's testimony from the trial transcript; more background might tell us more about him."

"I'm on it," Nate says.

"They're letting you out?"

"They're never letting me out; I think some secret hospital court has convicted me and sentenced me to life in here. But I'm making a break for it."

"Just take care of yourself," I say. "I'm going to follow Bettis anyway; the murder book is not that important."

Jessie leaves to start her stakeout at the auto dealership. I've told her that once Bettis is tucked away for the night, I'll come there and spell her.

Once she's gone, I ask Nate, "Are you okay?"

He shrugs. "They're worried that they can't get rid of the infection. They can't seem to figure out why."

"So just do what they say."

He changes the subject. "What's going on with you and Jess?"

"I'm crazy about her. But she's afraid that when I remember why I left her, I'll do it again."

"I believe I mentioned what would happen to you if you did that."

"You did, but it's something you and she don't need to worry about."

Before I leave, Nate calls the barracks to speak to Bettis. He does it on a pretext, basically so he can discover whether Bettis is there, so I'll be able to follow him. He also does it grudgingly, since he continues not to believe that Bettis could be guilty of the kind of things that I'm talking about.

I catch a break; Bettis is there but will be leaving to go out on patrol in forty-five minutes.

I head down to the barracks, waiting at a distance outside the parking lot until I see Bettis pull out. It'll probably be a waste of time for me, but I've got nothing better to do for the next thirty-four hours, which is when the deadline I gave Congers expires.

GHARSI WASN'T YET DONE, BUT HE WAS EXHAUSTED. The tension involved in working with powerful, volatile explosives is extraordinarily intense, and requires great concentration.

Gharsi was not simply filling each trunk with explosives. They had to be placed carefully and strategically, so that every inch of available space could be utilized. And then it had to be wired together, the most delicate part of the job. Then the timers had to be set, and it all had to be cushioned, so as to withstand the jostling of normal driving.

Although Gharsi was expert at it, and incredibly disciplined as far as the work was concerned, the sheer volume of it was draining. It moved slower than he had expected and hoped, but he had just finished the ninth of the twelve cars, so he would make his self-imposed deadline.

Luther Castle had been there with him most of the time, and had even offered to help in the process. But

Gharsi was rigid about it; he would do the work, that way there would be no chance of error.

Each car, when finished, was three times more powerful than any single ordnance dropped in World War II, with the exception of the atomic bombs. And each car, Gharsi knew, was fated to end up under an entire building's worth of rubble.

Castle kept Bennett informed periodically. His boss was anxious to know the progress, not because he had any particular interest in Gharsi's goals or actions, since the man would be dead soon anyway. But the sooner Gharsi was done, the sooner the money would be transferred. Bennett had a great deal of interest in the money.

Neither Gharsi nor Castle had any idea that Jessie was outside, observing the building from a secure vantage point, the same one that she and Doug used the last time they were there.

More importantly, Jessie had no way to know that Gharsi was inside, or that the explosives had made their way back to the building. She arrived long after he was in place, and he was in a closed garage-like room with the twelve cars.

As far as she could tell, it was a typical, if slow, day at the dealership. Occasionally customers would show up, but only a couple stayed long enough to possibly have bought a car. She saw no evidence that anything unusual or sinister was going on, because there was nothing to see.

Jessie had been on quite a few stakeouts in her career, and many of them had not borne fruit. But that was okay; she was used to it, and she was patient.

So she would watch, and wait.

Doug was also watching, but instead of being focused on a stationary building, he was observing Jerry Bettis, who was anything but stationary. It seemed as if Bettis was experiencing a typical tour for a detective. There was a stop to investigate an apparent domestic violence incident, and then a few visits to crime scenes, most likely burglaries.

Doug couldn't tell from a distance exactly what Bettis was doing at these places, but in each of them other cops were present. If Bettis was involved with anything related to Bennett or Gharsi, he was hiding it well.

Gnawing at Doug was the fact that he had no way of knowing if Congers had decided to act on the information he provided, but he had little confidence that it was happening. His threat to go public was not an empty one, nor was it an attempt to gain some kind of childish revenge for being ignored and disrespected.

If he was to actually go on television, there would undoubtedly be an intense reaction. The dealership in Garfield really would attract an amazing amount of attention, and Manhattan parking lots would probably institute substantially increased security measures, at least in the short term.

If nothing else, it would likely delay or cancel the planned operation. Of course, if nothing happened then Doug would look like a crackpot, but it would be more than worth the trade-off.

The decision was an easy one; Doug would follow through on his publicity threat if Congers did not do his part. Unfortunately, he didn't quite know how to do that;

he certainly couldn't call on Grant Friedman, the department publicist.

Doug remembered that he had the card from the *Today Show* booker, Lillian Singer, who had approached him on the street in Manhattan, offering him the opportunity to be interviewed at a time of his choosing. He had not given any interviews after the Trenton press conference, so he was still considered a sought-after interview, a big-time "get."

So he called her number, and told her assistant it was Doug Brock calling. He thought he might have to explain who he was, but within ten seconds Singer was on the phone, bubbling over with enthusiasm.

"I'm so glad you called," she enthused. "I hope you want to come on the show? We would LOVE to have you."

"I'd like to come on the day after tomorrow."

She was a little surprised by the specificity. "Is there anything particular you want to talk about, or just a general interview going over the recent events, and your memory loss . . . that kind of thing?"

"Well, I'd like to leave that open."

"What do you mean?"

"I might have some news to break, and if I do, it will be huge. If not, we can talk about whatever you want."

"Come on, you can't leave me hanging like that," she said.

"I'm afraid I have to. I won't know myself until probably tomorrow night."

"Okay, but please call me as soon as you can give me some more information."

"I will."

They went on to make the arrangements. He would arrive at six fifteen in the morning, and depending on the contents of the interview, it would air in either the first or second half hour. Singer made one more attempt to find out what was going on, but Doug again refused to answer.

It was the first and last thing of consequence that Doug accomplished that day. He followed Bettis home, and then met up with Jessie, who had nothing to report regarding activity at the used car place.

Maybe the next day would be different . . . maybe Congers and his people would do something. If not, Doug was prepared to go public and shake up the world.

SOMETIME DURING THE NIGHT, I MET DAVID TYREE.

I don't literally mean that I met him; what I actually did was remember him. Also Plaxico Burress. And Michael Strahan. And Eli Manning. And Steve Smith.

It's something that I can't explain. I went to sleep with no recollection of the Giants beating the Patriots in the Super Bowl, though I've read about it since. But during the night I relived it; the feelings I had watching it flooded back. It was like seeing it for the first time.

The catch David Tyree made in that game was and is the best I've ever seen, and that I could have forgotten it, whatever my injuries, is incomprehensible to me.

But the memory is back, and so are some others. Nothing else terribly significant, just some people I knew, movies I've seen, restaurants I've gone to. Nothing relating to Jessie, or Johnnie Arroyo, or Nicholas Bennett, or my shooting, or the current case. The recollection god is obviously out to torture me.

I stayed here at Jessie's last night. We didn't talk about it; it was just understood. It felt good that way, and comfortable. This morning I haven't mentioned David Tyree or any of the other things I've remembered, because I think my returning memory makes her worry about us, about the possibility of me connecting to why I left her the first time.

We can't think of anything better to do today than we did yesterday. That's not to say that what we did yesterday was particularly good; it was an absolute waste of time. But maybe today will be better, or maybe Congers will come up with something. If not, *Today Show* here I come.

"You want to switch off?" I ask. "Would you rather follow Bettis, while I watch the used car place?"

"No, thanks," she says. "Let's keep it this way."

"Because you think Bettis is clean, and that there's more chance of something happening at the car place."

She nods. "You got it."

Nate finds out for me that Bettis is not going on duty until two o'clock, and that seems a good enough time for Jessie to start her stakeout as well. So we're able to hang out at home and relax, before going on our way.

"Don't forget, anything unusual, please call me."

"You do the same," she says.

For the first couple of hours, Bettis spends his time again doing what seems like normal duty, nothing unusual or suspicious. I don't hear from Jessie, which doesn't worry me. She can handle herself, and would definitely call me and bring in backup if she were worried about anything taking place.

I'm not pleased that Bettis is heading south on the Garden State Parkway and seems to be going some distance. We're already at exit 141, which is almost fifteen miles from Garfield. I don't know how far he is going, or why, but the farther we go the longer it will take me to get back to Jessie if I need to.

Bettis takes me another five miles, gets off the parkway, and leads me on a winding road to a park set on a small lake. There are about thirty cars in the parking lot, but I don't see any people. I assume they are all near the lake picnicking and swimming. There are a lot of trees between the parking lot and the lake, so I'm not able to see from my vantage point.

Bettis gets out of the car and walks down the path through the trees, toward the lake. Perhaps there is some disturbance down there that has called for a police presence, but I certainly don't see any signs of it. We obviously have officers that work much closer to here, so Bettis should only have been sent here if a large force was required. But there are no other police cars, so it doesn't seem likely.

I park at the other side of the lot, also adjacent to the trees. I could stay here, where I'd be able to see Bettis when he returns to his car, without him noticing me. But his arrival here seems a little suspicious; I can't see why normal police work would have drawn him here. So I decide to follow him, maintaining a decent distance.

I take a different path through the trees, so that I won't run into him should he be returning to his car. I put my phone on vibrate, so that Bettis can't hear it ringing. The original path is in my sight line, so if I see him leaving, I can get back to my car and follow him.

The picnic and swimming areas are a couple of hundred yards away from the parking lot. I get to where I can see them, but so far there is no sign of Bettis. All of a sudden, I can feel the phone vibrating in my pocket, and the caller ID says it is Jessie. "Jess," I say, talking softly. "What's up?"

"Some people . . . men . . . have been showing up here. There's also customers arriving and leaving, but the men that have been coming in alone . . . I don't think they've been leaving, at least not in the cars that they came in."

"How many are we talking about?" I ask.

"It's hard to tell, because some could be customers, and some might be employees. But a good guess would be eight. They're arriving separately, maybe five or ten minutes apart. A few cars have also pulled out that I don't recognize. It could all be normal business, Doug, but I don't think so."

I am very unhappy about this turn of events. I'm far away, and standing in the middle of a park. It will take me a while to get to her. I certainly don't want to tell her to get closer or do anything that could put her in danger.

"Call Congers," I say. "Tell him what's going on; tell him you think they are Bennett's men."

"I shouldn't call Bradley?"

"Bradley's a waste of time; the most he might do is call Congers himself. Better it should come from you, because you're on the scene. Don't tell Congers I told you to call; that will just make him think it's a waste of time. Make up anything you want, but make sure he gets his ass down there, with a bunch of agents."

"Okay, Doug. I'm on it."

"I'll be there as soon as I can," I say, and I cut off the call.

I still don't see Bettis, but that's not high on my list of concerns right now. The two goons in the park told me that there was going to be a meeting of the guys that Bennett was recruiting, for huge money, and I'd bet a similar amount of money that that is what Jessie is watching.

I start back for the car on a run. If Bettis sees me, so be it. I reach the car and get in. I'm just about to turn the key in the ignition when I hear, "What the hell are you doing, Doug?"

The voice is coming from the backseat, and it belongs to Jerry Bettis. I see him in the rearview mirror; he is directly behind me. I can't see if he's holding a gun, but it certainly wouldn't surprise me.

"I came for a swim."

"Don't be a wiseass, Doug. You've been following me for two days; you must have forgotten how to do it without being noticed. You even let me lead you into this trap."

"Then you know what I've been doing. I've been following you." I've got to get away from him somehow, but it is not going to be easy, with him directly behind me inside my car.

"Why?" he asks.

"Because I think you're working with Nicholas Bennett. I think you're dirty, Jerry." I don't want to have a long conversation with him; I want to get to Jessie. I don't want to talk about how Bennett had to have found out from him that the *New York Times* story was wrong, because no further attempts were made on my life.

But then, just thinking about that triggers an even more frightening thought, something I hadn't realized before.

"You must have landed on your head harder than I thought," Bettis says. "Where the hell did you get that idea?"

I'm talking, but my mind is racing, and I'm just hoping that what I'm thinking is wrong. It has to be wrong. "Because somebody on the inside has known every move I've been making," I say, grasping at straws. "And you and Bennett set up Oscar Filion."

"Who is Oscar Filion?"

I have a feeling I'm being dragged to a place I don't want to be, a place that scares the shit out of me. "Jerry, you arrested a guy named Oscar Filion. You testified against him at trial."

"Oh, right," he says, remembering. "It was a murder case; he got convicted."

"You said at trial that there was an anonymous tip that came in, which provided the information that ultimately led to the arrest."

He takes a moment, thinking back. "Right."

"Who got the tip? Who took down the information?" I ask, knowing and dreading the answer.

"My partner; he did most of the legwork, but he was tied up on something, so I made the arrest. It was Dan Congers."

"Jerry, if you're not going to shoot me, get the hell out of the car."

JESSIE WAS SURPRISED AT THE REACTION SHE GOT *from Congers when she reached him.*

She expected some pushback, some skepticism, based on the waste of time that took place the first time agents were sent to the auto dealership.

Instead he listened to everything she had to say, and had only one question: "Did Doug tell you to call?"

"No," she said, "I haven't spoken to him about this. He's not reachable right now."

"Okay," Congers said. "I'm not far from there. I'll be right over, and then we can assess what kind of manpower we'll need."

She told him where she was, but she didn't have to because he already knew from last time. And he didn't mention that the reason he wasn't far away is that he was already headed there.

He arrived in less than five minutes, and she got out of her car to greet him. Before she could tell him what was going on in more detail, he said, "Come on, get in my car and let's see what's going on."

She got in the passenger seat, and they drove over to the dealership and parked in the back. "Let's go in," he said.

His approach surprised her; they could be walking into a dangerous situation. "Just like that?" she asked.

"Just like that, Jessie," he said, the gun already in his hand. "Just like that."

I COULD HAVE EXPLAINED TO BETTIS WHAT WAS GOING ON.

It would have taken some time, which I don't have. He might have believed me, but more likely he wouldn't. If he did, he could have called Captain Bradley and tried to convince him to send officers to Garfield. Maybe Bradley would have believed him and sprung into action, but more likely not.

But those details are only part of the reason why I didn't tell him, and not the major part. I'm afraid that Jessie is in danger, and officers descending on the place would increase that danger.

The first thing I do is call her, but she doesn't answer the call. It could be that she's gotten out of the car to get a closer look at the building, and left her phone behind. But I don't believe that for a minute, and it leaves me with a cold chill of fear.

I briefly consider calling Bradley myself, but reject the idea for the same reason I didn't have Bettis do it. If he didn't believe me, it would accomplish nothing. If he did, and sent officers, the outcome might be worse.

I call Nate in the hospital. I'm afraid he might have been released, and I don't even remember his cell phone number. But he answers the hospital phone, and when he does, I say, "Nate, I'm glad you're still there."

"Thanks a lot. The damn infection is getting worse, and—"

I interrupt. "Nate, let me do the talking; this is important." I go on to tell him the situation, and conclude with, "If you don't hear from me in an hour, call Bradley and convince him to send in the troops."

"Got it," he says. "What are you going to do?"

"Beats the hell out of me."

It's going to take me at least another twenty minutes to reach the auto dealership, which is going to be the longest twenty minutes of my life. I was telling Nate the truth; I have no idea what will be waiting for me, or how I will deal with it.

When I finally get there, I drive past the place where I know Jessie should be. Her car is there, but she is not. If there was the slightest spark of hope left that I was wrong, that extinguishes it.

I continue driving, and pull into a diner's parking lot about three hundred yards down the road. I park and place a call to Congers at his office, since I don't have his cell phone number.

"This is Doug Brock," I say to the person who answers the phone. "I need to speak to Lieutenant Congers."

"I'm sorry, he's out."

"I lost his cell phone number, so please patch me through to him," I say.

"I can't do that."

"It's very important. If you reach him, he will want to talk to me."

There is a hesitation, and then the woman says, "Hold on, please." After a couple of nervous minutes, she says, "Lieutenant Congers is on the line."

"Brock, what is it now?" he asks.

"I'm just checking in to see where you stand on what we talked about," I say.

"That's it? That's what was so important?"

"It's very important, although maybe to me more than you."

He sighs an exaggerated sigh. "All right, when I get back to the office, I'll check on the progress, and get back to you."

"I have an interview scheduled with the *Today Show* tomorrow morning."

"Good for you," he says, just before disconnecting the call.

"I'll be seeing you soon, asshole," is what I say to the dead phone.

The call has removed any doubt that Congers is at the auto dealership. If he wasn't, he would have made some reference to the fact that Jessie had called him. The fact that he didn't means that he is not being upfront with me, and the only possible reason for that is that he is on the other side.

He has Jessie, and they are in that building. One way or the other, I'm going to be joining them.

NINE OF THE TWELVE EXPLOSIVE-FILLED CARS HAD *already left the building.*

The other three were ready to do so, their drivers behind their respective wheels. They were spacing it out and leaving at five-minute intervals; a caravan pulling out at once might have attracted attention, were anybody watching. Each time one was ready to go, the large door opened, and closed after the car departed.

In an office adjacent to the room with the remaining cars were Nicholas Bennett, Luther Castle, and Ahmat Gharsi. The outside of the office was glass, so they could see out into the garage area. The men sat at a small table, empty except for a landline telephone that was in front of Bennett.

Bennett had asked Gharsi once again to go over the timing of the events to follow, so that they could know what to expect, and have time to cement alibis.

"Assuming your people return and report that their missions went as expected, I will confirm at least a few of those reports by personally inspecting them. Then, at midnight, I will dial a number. The receipt of that phone call will trigger the first of the explosions."

"And the others?"

"There is a different cell number for each. I will dial them, three minutes apart, which will detonate them one at a time," Gharsi said. Some of what he said was not true and was said for Bennett's benefit, so that he would not attempt to interfere with anything before the remainder of the drivers were on their way.

The phone rang, and Bennett quickly answered it. He simply said the word "Nicholas," and then was quiet as he listened to the caller. When he hung up the phone, he said, "The money has been received." Then he allowed himself a small smile. "Excellent."

The door opened, and Congers came in with Jessie, his gun nestled in her back. The three men's faces registered their surprise, and Gharsi asked, "What is this?"

"This," Congers said, "is evidence that you people are not careful enough. She is a police officer. I would introduce you all to her, but she won't be alive long enough for you to establish much of a relationship."

"And who are you?" Gharsi asked.

Bennett answered the question. "He's the man who made all this possible."

I AM GOING TO NEED SOME HELP.

Approaching the used car dealership by myself is too risky; there is far too great a likelihood that I will be detected. If there is still a chance to save Jessie, that would destroy it.

I go into the diner, and let my eyes scan the place. There are six tables occupied, three by groups including kids, one by an older woman sitting alone, one with a couple in at least their late seventies, and one by three guys that if they're not truck drivers, they should be.

An easy call.

I walk over to the table with the three guys and sit down with them, clearly surprising them in the process. "Do any of you guys recognize me?" I ask.

Two of them reflexively shake their head, but the third guy is clearly trying to place me. "Yeah, you're that cop, right? The one who shot that guy in the theater."

"That's me. I need one of you to help me. It's a matter of life and death."

The two that didn't recognize me don't seem thrilled

by the prospect, perhaps focusing on the "death" part of my request. But the third guy seems amenable. "What do I have to do?"

"What's your name?"

"People call me TJ."

"TJ, all you have to do is drive me over to that used car place down the road, park, and start to go in as if you're interested in buying a car. They're not open, so you turn around, get back in your car, and drive away."

"That's it?"

I nod. "That's it, and if you do it I'll take you on the *Today Show* with me tomorrow morning."

"No shit?"

"No shit," I confirm.

"You gotta work tomorrow," one of TJ's buddies says.

TJ shakes his head. "That ain't happenin' . . . I'm goin' on TV."

"You ready?" I ask. When he nods, I say, "Let's go."

We go out in the parking lot, and I tell him that we'll take his car. It turns out he has a covered pickup truck, which is even better. I quickly re-explain what he is to do, and he nods and says, "I got it."

He pulls up close to the building, near the end on the right side as we face it. It shields me from anyone seeing me when I get out the passenger side, while he gets out on the driver's side. He walks left toward the entrance to the showroom, while I go right, along the wall, to loop around toward the back.

The dealership is closed; it's after hours and the gathering darkness is a plus. All TJ is supposed to do is try the door, pretend to determine that it is locked, then get back in his truck and leave.

I know the inside of the building from having been in there when we were conducting the search. I'm sure the room that had the dozen cars in it is the one that the drivers are leaving from, although I don't know if they've all left. More importantly, I don't know if that's where Jessie is.

I can't stay out here too long; eventually I'll be seen. But I also cannot go bursting in without any idea of what I'm bursting in to. I press my ear up against the wall, and dial Jessie's cell phone. I can hear it ringing, and it sounds like it's off to the right, which is where an adjacent office is. She's either in that room, or near it. The call goes unanswered.

Suddenly the garage door opens and a car comes out. I hide against the wall and peer through the open door. The driver doesn't see me, because I'm on his passenger side, and he seems very focused on his driving. With his cargo, I don't blame him.

In the brief instant I have, I see that there is one car remaining in the room. I also catch a glimpse of a group of people in the office, since its outside wall is glass. I can only identify some of them quickly in the moment; I see Bennett, and Congers.

And just before the door closes again, I see Jessie.

"SO WHERE DO WE STAND?" CONGERS ASKED.

Luther Castle was the one who answered. "The last car is about to leave."

"Perfect. And when do the fireworks go off?"

"Gharsi will start making the phone calls at midnight tonight, setting them off one by one."

Congers turned to Bennett. "And the money?"

"Received."

"You did a beautiful job," Congers said. "It couldn't have worked out better."

"As I predicted," Bennett said.

"You really did. I've got to hand it to you. You, me, and all your people wind up rich, I become a national hero for stopping the worst attack ever planned on our mainland, and the only unfortunate loss of life is our lady friend and this terrorist." He pointed to Gharsi as he said it.

"What is he talking about?" Gharsi asked, turning to Bennett.

Bennett didn't respond to him, but instead turned to Castle. "Luther?"

Gharsi turned to look at Castle, who was pointing a gun at him. He didn't react to the threat in any way, even as Bennett said, "You are in over your head here, my friend."

Congers said, "Let's not move too hastily. Are we sure we know where the cars are going to be parked?"

"Luther chose the exact places himself," Bennett said, and then turned to Gharsi. "Time to die, my friend; it's been very profitable knowing you."

"Hold it," Congers said, looking out into the area where the cars were parked. "Wait until the last car leaves. No sense having an additional witness."

Almost on cue, the large door slowly opened, and the last car pulled out. "Now you may kill him," Congers said.

Castle raised his gun, but then turned and put a bullet in the center of Congers's forehead. He turned again and pointed the gun at his boss, Bennett. "Well, Nicholas . . . I now have control over the organization, and the bank account, which is quite full right now. You've taught me well."

He slowly readied to pull the trigger, pointing the gun at Bennett's head. "Consider this a forced retirement, a changing of the guard."

THE DOOR OPENS, AND THE LAST CAR PULLS OUT.

There is no question that this represents my best, and probably only, chance to get into the building undetected. As the car moves out, I move in, then inch along the wall and crouch behind a pile of tires.

As soon as I do, I hear the shot.

I look toward the room, and see Luther Castle holding a gun, apparently just having fired it. A body is lying on the floor; I can't tell who it is, but I no longer see Congers. I think the man next to him is Gharsi, who has miraculously come back to life.

Across from them is Bennett, seated in a chair, and Jessie is standing against the wall. I think I hear a loud crashing noise from somewhere either on the other side of the building or outside. The people in the room react slightly to it as well, but not enough to make them go to see what it was.

I start to inch toward the room, my gun drawn. I need to get a better angle if I'm going to fire into the room, but I don't see how. At best I'll be able to get one of them, but I have no way to prevent one of the remaining two from shooting Jessie.

Just as I'm getting into a better position, I see Castle raise his gun slightly and fire. Jessie goes down, but the motion isn't that of a person who has been shot. I believe she is diving under the table; at least that's what I want to believe.

I see Bennett slump and then roll off his chair onto the floor; he is the one that Castle shot. I don't take the time to ponder why he did that, I just take two shots at Castle. He grabs for his neck, and I see blood spurting through his hands. I'm not sure if the second bullet hit him or not, but I don't think it's going to matter.

Gharsi dives under the table as well, and I cringe as I listen for the sound of him possibly shooting Jessie. But instead there is no sound at all; seconds tick away as I try and figure out what to do next.

"Gharsi!" I yell. "Throw out your gun and come out of there; it's your only chance to get out alive."

And he does come out a few seconds later, but he's still holding his gun. Even worse is the fact that he is holding Jessie by the neck, pushing her in front of him, as a shield.

"Where are you, my friend?" Gharsi asks. "You want to come out, or perhaps watch her die from your hiding place, like a coward?"

I have no idea what to do; if I've been trained to handle situations like this in the past ten years, it's a memory my mind hasn't recovered yet.

Gharsi starts to move toward the showroom, holding Jessie between himself and where he knows I must be hiding. If I stand and show myself, I won't have a clear shot at him. He can shoot me, and then Jessie. If I do nothing, and he gets away with her, she has no chance to survive. I cannot come up with an option that leaves her alive.

I stand up and slowly walk toward them. I can't let her die without trying to do something. My gun is pointed at Gharsi, and his is now pointed at me. The problem is that Jessie is acting as his shield. I want to shoot, but I can't pull the trigger, because I will almost definitely hit her.

Gharsi smiles. "You made the wrong choice, my friend. You could have lived."

I have no place to move, and still no way to shoot him without hitting Jessie. I see him aim at me and start to pull the trigger.

Then I see his head explode.

Then I see Nate, at the showroom door, lowering his handgun.

"I told you I could shoot," he says.

BRADLEY, METCALF, AND A WHOLE BUNCH OF COPS SHOW *up a few minutes later.*

Metcalf takes one look at the bodies and says, "Talk to me. Do not leave out a thing."

"No time for that now," I say. "There are twelve cars, fully loaded with explosives, sitting in parking lots under buildings in Manhattan."

"What will detonate them?" he asks.

Jessie says, "Gharsi claimed that it would be by cell phone calls, which he was going to make at midnight."

Metcalf looks at Gharsi lying on the floor with half a head. "He's not going to be making any calls."

"That doesn't matter," Jessie says, "because he was lying. They have to be set on timers."

"Why do you say that?"

"Because there is no cell phone service in those lots, not on those floors. We know that, and Gharsi was too smart not to have known it."

"Why would he lie about that?"

"I'll give you my best guess," I say. "I think he knew

there was a chance he could get killed, and he wanted everyone to think that the danger was contained. I think the mission was more important to him than his life."

"Do we know where they are?"

"We know exactly where they are," Jessie says, and she and I start writing out lists, while Metcalf alerts what seems like every bomb squad in the western hemisphere.

Jessie, Nate, and I are there for another three hours, being debriefed and describing everything that has happened tonight, in excruciating detail. It is only later that we hear about the incredible operation that the Joint Terrorism Task Force, in tandem with the New York City Police, conducted.

They evacuated all twelve buildings, identified the cars, and rendered them harmless. All were set to go off, not at midnight, but at nine o'clock in the morning, when the greatest loss of human life would occur.

Then they began the process of rounding up the twelve drivers, some of whom had mistakenly returned to the auto dealership, not realizing they were surrendering in the process. Eight were taken into custody immediately, but the other four were soon to follow.

As he did after the theater shooting, Metcalf conducts the final interview. His last question to me is, "How did you know about Congers?"

"A few reasons," I say. "For one, they tried to kill me after the *New York Times* story said I was getting my memory back, and after I told Bradley and Bettis it wasn't true. But once I told Congers the truth, they stopped going after me. And after I told Congers about the two guys in the park, they turned up dead. Bennett must have known that they talked, and Congers must have told them."

"Anything else?" Metcalf asks.

I nod. "Bettis told me that Congers reported Tony Gibbons at the pier was clean, but I knew he wasn't. Congers denied telling him that, but he was lying. And he's also the one who got the explosives hidden before our search of the used car lot, because Bradley told him what was going on the night before.

"One more thing," I say. "Remember that original phone call to Nate I made just before I got shot? I said, 'Find Congers and—' before I got cut off. Well, I think I know how I was going to finish that sentence. I was going to say 'Find Congers and arrest him.' "

"You're not a bad cop," he says. "Maybe the thing at the theater wasn't luck after all."

"I'm all tingly; I live for your praise," I say.

I finally walk out of the dealership with Jessie and Nate. Nate says, "I'll see you guys later. I'd better get back to the hospital, but I want to stop and get a pastrami sandwich on the way."

"You weren't released?" I ask.

"Nah. I've still got the infection." He smiles. "Doesn't hurt my shooting any."

"How'd you know where in the building we were?" I ask.

"TJ told me," he says, and points to my loyal helper, standing in the parking lot.

I walk over to TJ. "You okay?"

"Are you kidding? This was the most fun I've ever had."

"Where do you live?"

He gives me his address, and I tell him, "I'll pick you up at five thirty; you're going to be on television."

IT'S BEEN ALMOST A MONTH SINCE THAT NIGHT.

The *Today Show* was just the beginning, though it was quite a beginning. I read the other day that it was the highest rated show they've ever done, and they milked the interview by spreading it out over three days.

I've pretty much stayed out of the limelight as much as I can, but it's not easy. I'm mobbed everywhere I go; people mean well, but it's exhausting. TJ's liking it considerably more than me; he's done his own media tour.

Nate is out of the hospital, as the infection was finally conquered. He's also gotten more than his share of deserved media recognition, but what he is most pleased about is losing eleven pounds while in the hospital. The fact that it took him about an hour and a half to gain it back hasn't seemed to dampen his enthusiasm.

I was able to finally give Jessie the recognition she deserved in the *Today Show* interview. She's using it to force her way back onto the street, leaving the cyber-crime area to others.

Captain Bradley thinks I've had enough time to recuperate and wants me back on the job full time, but I've told him I need some time to think, which is what I'm doing now. On some level I don't want to return at all; I want to put all of this behind me. But I'm a cop, that's what I do, and I think I'll probably start doing it again.

Just not right now.

Some of my memory has come back. It seemed like it was going to return chronologically, but it hasn't; things have been just popping up at random. I still have no recollection of being shot, or the events leading up to it, and that doesn't bother me.

Been there, done that.

About two weeks ago I remembered Johnnie Arroyo. I've never experienced anything like that moment, and I don't recommend it to anyone. Within a few seconds, I met and got to know a young man, loved him like my son, and watched him get shot to death. The first time it happened, in real time, it sent me into a tailspin, and I believe that knowledge is helping me to avoid a similar descent the second time around.

I also remember the sequence of events and feelings that followed, and which led me to break off my relationship with Jessie, and the rest of the world as well. It's very painful, both the feelings themselves, and especially the knowledge of how I acted when I felt them.

At first I wasn't going to tell her that those memories had returned, but then I realized that I had to. So I shared it all.

When I did, she came over to me, standing maybe

five inches in front of me. "You don't have to stay," she said.

"I know."

"You need to do what feels right for you."

"I know," I said.

"But whatever you are going to do, whatever you decide, you need to do it now."

"I know."

"Just to be clear, if you say 'I know' again, I am going to knee you in the groin."

"I didn't know that," I said, and then I kissed her and told her I love her, and that I am very, very thankful for a second chance.

"I know," she said.

Also by David Rosenfelt

Thrillers

Without Warning
Airtight
Heart of a Killer
On Borrowed Time
Down to the Wire
Don't Tell a Soul

Andy Carpenter Novels

Who Let the Dog Out?
Hounded
Unleashed
Leader of the Pack
One Dog Night
Dog Tags
New Tricks
Play Dead
Dead Center
Sudden Death
Bury the Lead
First Degree
Open and Shut
OutFoxed

Nonfiction

Lessons from Tara: Life Advice from the World's Most Brilliant Dog
Dogtripping: 25 Rescues, 11 Volunteers, and 3 RVs on Our Canine Cross-Country Adventure